BEECH BANK GIRLS II

Beech Bank Girls II

Making A Difference

ELEANOR WATKINS

DERNIER PUBLISHING
Tonbridge

First published 2010

Published by Dernier Publishing
P.O. Box 403, Tonbridge TN9 9BJ, England
www.dernierpublishing.com

ISBN: 978 0 9536963 7 6

Book design and production for the publisher by
Bookprint Creative Services, <www.bookprint.co.uk>
Printed in Great Britain.

To my six great-nieces;
Saffron, Megan, Charlotte, Rhian,
Teagan and Elin, with my love

Contents

PART ONE

Rachel's Story

NEW BEGINNINGS

one

That week didn't exactly get off to a good start in several ways. I wasn't in a very good mood to begin with, if I'm honest. Getting ready for school Monday morning, first day back after the October half-term, my head was still reeling with the news we'd been told the night before.

It was one of the weekends that the step-siblings – all four of them – had come to stay. Maxwell is a year younger than me, 13, the twins Ben and Jade nearly 11, and Billie is seven. With my sister Ruth, 12, my mum and step-dad Ted, not to mention the pets, we're quite a houseful.

But we'd had a good time that weekend. No quarrels to speak of, no major differences, no accidents, nobody going down with a sore throat or a sniffle or coming out in a rash. (Except for one annoying spot that appeared on my chin.) We'd gone out into the countryside on Saturday, walked the dog in the woods all in autumn colours, with piles of fallen leaves crackling under our feet and the smell of damp earth and wood smoke from someone's bonfire. Mum and Ted were holding hands and looking soppy, the kids were kicking leaves about and climbing trees, and we had lunch at a pub. I had quite an interesting conversation with Max about earthworms. He's coming on a lot, that boy!

Then on Sunday we had a morning in the garden and a barbecue and bonfire after church. Ted has to take the Steps back to their grandparents on Sunday evening, and they were just about packed and ready when Mum asked us all to come into the sitting room for a moment as they had something to tell us. We all trooped in, quieter than usual. The last time this had happened it had been to break the news of the death of the Steps' mother, Ted's first wife. It had happened only weeks ago and was fresh in all of our minds. Surely something else bad couldn't have happened?

But Mum and Ted didn't look sad at all. In fact, both of them had big grins. They looked at each other and then at us.

"We wanted to tell you when you were all here together," began Mum, and was interrupted by several voices.

"Tell us what?"

"Is it a surprise?"

"Are we going to Disneyworld?" This from Billie, who is crazy about princesses, fairies and magical castles.

Ted shook his head. "'Fraid not, sweetie. Not any time soon, at least."

"Are we getting a pony?" asked Ruth hopefully.

"Not a pony," said Mum tantalisingly, and then, as though she couldn't hold it in any longer, she burst out, "We are getting something wonderful, though! A baby!"

For a moment there was just a kind of stunned silence. I looked round at the other faces. Max had a kind of puzzled expression, as though he hadn't worked out that when people are married they sometimes have babies. Ruth's mouth had fallen open into a round O shape and her eyes were out on stalks. Ben looked faintly embarrassed and I saw for a moment a flicker of disappointment cross Jade's face. She and Ruth would have been in their element if we'd really been getting a pony! Billie looked completely bewildered. She'd been the baby for so long that she probably didn't know what to think. I sympathised totally. Whatever I'd been expecting, it certainly wasn't this. I didn't know what to think either.

The silence lasted only a second or two, but it seemed longer. Mum and Ted were looking round at us, eagerly waiting for our reactions, holding their breath almost.

Then Max seemed to pull himself together and he smiled in what seemed to be a totally genuine way. Trust him to do the right thing! He could always be a bit of a creep! For one awful moment I thought he was going to shake Ted by the hand! But he just gave them both a hug and said, "Well, congratulations."

Mum and Ted both looked relieved. Ruth closed her mouth, blinked a couple of times and then did the same. A sudden buzz of chatter broke out among the others.

"Will it be a boy? We've got enough girls in this family!"

"Where will it sleep?"

"Will it be here for Christmas?"

"Can I push it in the pram?"

Mum was laughing and doing her best to answer. The baby would be here around the end of May, she said. I could see she and Ted were both as pleased as punch. Then she looked over the heads of the others and caught my eye.

"What do you think, Rachel?"

Well, I didn't quite mean to, but I was still so gobsmacked I said the first thing that came into my head. My mind was a turmoil of shock, dismay, doubt and something that might just have been fear. I heard myself say, in horribly prim-sounding tones, "But you can't have a baby, Mum! I mean, you're 40! Forty plus!"

Her smile slipped a little, but she said, "Don't be silly! Lots and lots of women have babies in their forties these days. It's quite safe, and I'm fit as a fiddle." Her eyes pleaded with me to be pleased for them both, but I pretended not to see. Something was always happening to spoil things. My dad had died. I'd had awful trouble getting used to the Steps at first, especially Max. Then their mum had died. Things had been just beginning to get better. And now this! The last thing I wanted was a crying, demanding, smelly baby in the house. We were crowded enough as it was. And she needn't expect me to change nappies or push it round in the pram! People might think it was mine!

I didn't say any of this. I even managed to apologise, and say I was pleased too, lying through my teeth.

There was a lot more hugging and kissing, and chattering and laughing, and the Steps were a whole hour late starting for home. I went off to my room, and was glad that Ruth wouldn't be sharing with me tonight, now that the others had gone. Not that it made any difference though, because she came in right after me to pick up some of her stuff. She sat down on the other bed and I could see she wanted to discuss this turn of events.

"It's exciting, isn't it? This baby will really be related to every one of us. It'll kind of link us all together, won't it?"

"Yeah, yeah," I said grumpily, rummaging in my school bag. "If you don't mind, I've got homework to do."

"You can't have. We did it all before the weekend. But if you're in a mood, I'll go. You could act a bit more pleased though. Mum and Ted are really happy."

Ruth is two years younger than me but sometimes she's a lot more sensible. Often nicer too, I have to admit. She went off and I picked up my mobile. It was too late to call all my mates, but I might catch one or two of them. Texting wouldn't be quite the same, I wanted to hear a sympathetic voice. I tried Willow first but she was in the bath. Then Amber, who I thought might understand because her mum had her little sister when most of her kids were almost grown up. I must have been mumbling, because Amber misheard me and almost burst my eardrum with a loud shriek.

"PREGNANT? You're PREGNANT?"

Amber is a terrible drama queen and so is Ruth, though Mum says I can put on a pretty good performance myself when I want to. I quickly set her straight.

"Not me, you dork! My mum. My mum's pregnant. Can you believe it?"

If I'd expected understanding and sympathy, I didn't get it. Amber thought the whole thing was hilarious and couldn't stop laughing. When she began picturing the child as a kind of mini-Maxwell, I knew it was time to say goodnight, switch off the phone and go to bed.

The perfect ending to a lovely weekend – not.

two

Our house seemed very quiet next morning, the inhabitants being reduced by half when the Steps left. Ted leaves for work early, Ruth had the morning off because of a dentist appointment, which would normally mean a lie-in for her, although I'd heard her go up and down the stairs earlier. No sign of Mum. I had the half-resentful thought that she can't even be bothered to see me off to school any more.

I was pouring cereal when Ruth came bursting in, switched on the kettle and popped bread into the toaster. "Mum isn't too good. Morning sickness. It'll pass, she says. I'm taking her up some tea and toast in bed."

Well, wonderful! And trust Ruth to be the thoughtful one. I crunched cornflakes while she prepared a tray like a proper little nurse, and went upstairs with it. I called goodbye to them both and left.

Winter was nearly here now, the nice weekend giving place to grey and overcast, like my mood, with a smell of earth and damp leaves. Chilly too. I was glad of my warm jacket this morning. Ruth and I used to walk to school; the High School is 20 minutes or so away, as we're right on the edge of town, almost in the country. Mum would drive us if we were late, or the weather was absolutely foul.

Now, though, things have changed, and there's a school bus – a minibus, to be exact. This is mainly because of the large numbers of immigrant families who are in the area, some all the year round but lots more in summer and autumn when they come for the fruit and potato picking. A bus is laid on for bringing their children to school from the large camps on some of the farms and, as there were spare seats, those of us along the route are picked up too.

Our drive is long and winding, a country lane really. Lots of potholes needing attention, as Ted had remarked at the weekend. I mooched along, hands in pockets, and pondered my reaction to the news of the impending new addition to the family. The others all seemed pleased and excited. Whatever was wrong with me? Was I jealous? Hardly, with six kids already in the family! Embarrassed? A little, maybe . . . I'd have got over that though.

The inconvenience? Well, we have a big house but it's already bursting at the seams at times, what with the kids, our Labrador Henry, the cat Poppy, the turtle Timmy and Ben's hamster, which travels back and forth with him. One small baby wouldn't make that much difference, although they do seem to need an awful lot of equipment for such small people. I quite like babies, actually. Me and the girls often babysit for our vicar and his wife. That wasn't it either.

I suddenly realised what the problem was, just as I tripped at the edge of a pothole and almost went flying. I got my balance just in time with a sigh of relief, no fall and therefore no holes in my tights. As I shouldered my bag again, I realised I was lonely.

Now I'm certainly not a saddo with no friends. Just the opposite. I have really good mates I can trust and I'm a sociable kind of person. People are drawn to me, that's what Sadie, our youth leader, says, and I think it's true. I like meeting people and being friendly and having a good laugh and a bit of fun. Ted's kids like me and we get on, even Max these days.

But things have changed too. After Dad died, Mum, Ruth and I were a tight little group until Ted came along. As the elder one, Mum talked to me a lot, discussed things, told me how she felt. That doesn't happen much any more. Ted's the one she shares with, and the others all take her time and attention too. My sister and I used to be close but now Ruth's palled up with Jade. I miss them both, especially Mum. And when she has a new baby, well, I'll be way down her list of priorities.

In this self-pitying mood I waited for the bus at the end of the road, and reflected gloomily that it was late again. There'd be no time for any goss with the girls before class, no chance of unburdening myself and maybe getting rid of some of the gloom. It would be straight into registration, and then Maths first period, my fave subject, not.

The bus came, I got on and sat in a seat by myself, not in the mood for chat. Nobody my year on it anyway, at least, no girls. Two or three local boys travel on the bus, sitting in the back seats and mostly making a lot of noise. The migrant workers' kids are quiet; if they talk at all it's in their own languages. In any supermarket or town centre round here you hear a whole load of Eastern European languages – Polish, Romanian, Bulgarian and others. I've even learned to recognise one or two.

I noticed a couple of new kids today, a small boy sitting with the other migrant boys and a girl about my age on her own towards the front. She had long brown hair and looked shy, keeping her head well down. I was just wondering if she spoke any English, when one of the boys from the back came and plonked down beside me. It was Dean Perryman from my year, a short lad no taller than me (I would give anything to have longer legs), and a bit on the cheeky side. I edged towards the window and gave him an enquiring stare.

"Hiya," he said, "Good weekend?"

I nodded. What was he after? Surely he didn't fancy me? Wasting his time there, if so.

He came to the point. "It's, like, my mate. Russ."

I knew Russell Tripp, also in our year. He was one of those on the back of the bus.

"What about him?"

"Well – he wonders if you'd go out with him."

I heaved a sigh. What idiotic creatures boys can be! All the same, I couldn't resist half-turning to sneak a glance at Russell. He's a bit gingery, not bad looking but not my type at all. He was pretending to stare out of the window, trying to look nonchalant. Idiot! Then I saw that he had a spot right on his nose, and I felt a tinge of sympathy for him. My own spot was only just beginning to disappear.

I sighed again, and Dean looked encouraged. "Was that a yes or a no?"

"It's a maybe. And next time he wants to ask something, tell him to send the organ-grinder and not the monkey."

Dean snickered and went back to report to his mate. There was more snickering and some friendly punching of each other.

The moment the words were out of my mouth I could have kicked myself. I had no possible interest in Russell Tripp and no intention whatever of going out with him. What on earth had I been thinking? I'd have to find some way of wriggling out of it.

To cover my embarrassment, I got up and went to sit beside the new girl. She looked surprised but moved up to make room for me. I said, "You're new, aren't you? Where are you from?"

She seemed taken aback, as though she did not quite understand. I repeated, more slowly, "Which country do you come from?"

She understood now. "Ah. I come from Romania."

Romania. I knew vaguely where that was on the map. A very backward country, I remembered, very poor, lots of children who had been badly treated in orphanages when they were little. Did they still have those orphanages? Or were the children all grown up now? Maybe this girl was an orphan. She certainly didn't look very well off, in an old-fashioned kind of long bunchy skirt and a faded anorak. She'd get picked on pretty soon if she wasn't careful. Our school has a strict policy for dealing with bullying, but the migrant children came in for a lot of sly harassment all the same.

She seemed half-scared already, looking uncertainly at me from big brown eyes. I tried to be reassuring. "You'll like our school. It's nice. Do you have brothers and sisters?"

She understood that all right. "Ah, yes. Four. Younger ones. But not here." She held up four fingers. I wondered why she was not with her family.

"That's nice," I said lamely. "Maybe you'll be in my year at school."

She looked blank. "Year?"

"Yes. I'm in Year Nine."

"But – you are not nine years old?"

"No, no, it doesn't mean that. It's the number of years you've been in school."

Her puzzlement was growing. With some relief I saw

that we were pulling into the school car park. I jumped up. "They'll soon get you sorted. Maybe see you later."

She was swallowed up by the other migrant children as we got off the bus, and I hurried over to join Amber and Chloe who'd been waiting for me. It was only later that I realised I hadn't asked the girl's name.

three

Her name was Madalina. I'd discovered that by the end of the first period. I'd been right, she was in my year and she'd been put into our class. As it happened, she was the only Eastern European girl in our class, so the others and I thought we'd make a special effort to be friends with her. Didn't quite work out though, she gravitated to the other migrant kids from other classes at break time, even though they were all boys, and they stuck together in a group. Never mind, maybe I'd get a chance to get to know her on the bus.

Not today though. Me and my friends were all off to the Beech Bank Club after school. The BB is a cool club held in our local community centre, open every day after school and sometimes weekends too. It has just everything – a bistro-type coffee bar, computer room, games hall, quiet room, chill-out space. It's run by our vicar and his wife, a cool young(ish) couple who really like kids our age. I wonder how ever we managed before we had BB.

All my special mates went that afternoon, walking down together in a group from school. Only five of us at the mo though, as Holly has taken off to visit her cousin Sarah in Australia.

"Wonder how Holls is doing," said Amber as we set off. "Still can't get used to her not being here. Haven't heard a peep from her, not even a text or something on Chatspace."

"Oh yes, that reminds me," said Willow. "I got an email, to all of us really, saying she misses us but she's having a humungously good time."

"Lucky her," said Amber. "They didn't waste much time going to visit, did they? Sarah's only been gone a few months."

"It's because they wanted to avoid the really hot weather," said Willow. "Her mum can't stand the heat apparently. By Christmas it would be the middle of summer in Oz, baking hot."

Willow is kind of the leader of our group. For one thing, she's about six inches taller than the rest of us and looks older. She's really slim, has this creamy skin and fiery red hair and the kind of style that makes people turn round in the street for a second look. So she's well confident and able to be in control of things – for instance, she sometimes leads the Enquirers' class at BB, which is a group for people wanting to know more about what it means to be a Christian. Willow can be a bit bossy and usually thinks she's right, which is all the more annoying because usually she is.

But it was nice to have news of Holly, even though I

did think she could have emailed all of us and not just Willow. Truth to tell, I was still a bit peeved about the situation at home, and it was rubbing off on everything else.

"You OK, Rach?" Chloe asked as we went through the little gate into the community centre yard. Chloe is the sensitive one of our group, always able to spot if someone is bothered by something. She's the only blonde one of us, but doesn't act blonde at all – she's very bookish and wants to be a writer one day.

The other three had gone on ahead, so I told Chloe a bit about the way I was feeling about our family situation. The others had all thought it was wonderful news, and hinted that I must be a mean old grouch for not being over the moon. Chloe didn't though. She could sense I wasn't happy, and said quickly, "Tell you what, give me a buzz at home later. Then we can talk properly." And she reached out and gave my hand a squeeze as we went into the centre.

We chilled out for a bit over coffee, and listened to some music. Rod (our vicar) wasn't there, but his wife Sadie was. Rod's a twenty-first-century, hands-on dad, and was minding their two kids at home. Sadie was busy, flitting from one room to another, but stopped by our table for a minute. She was wearing an awesome dress-over-leggings outfit that looked like a million dollars but probably came from a charity shop. Sadie's like Willow, skinny, long legs, even a bin liner would look good on her.

"I hope you're all going to be here Friday evening," she said. "It's going to be special."

We pricked up our ears. "How do you mean, like, special?" asked Amber.

"Guest speaker – or more than one. I think you'll find them – challenging," she said mysteriously. We wanted more details but she smiled and would say no more. She'd got us intrigued though. We speculated for a while over the coffee mugs. Willow thought it might be a well-known youth leader. Annie and Chloe had visions of a rock band like Delirious?, though maybe a little less famous.

"Sadie said 'him' so we know at least it's a guy," said Amber. But then Annie pointed out that what she'd actually said was "them". We argued in a friendly way and fantasised pleasantly until it was time to go home.

Mum didn't appear again next morning. She'd seemed fine the night before, cooking our tea as usual and very happy and jokey. I did notice a little frown between her eyes once or twice when she looked at me, though. I tried to act normal, as though I hadn't got this big knot of misery inside me, but she can see through me, can Mum. She knows I can act cheerful on the outside when I'm anything but. And the stupid thing was, I couldn't seem to get myself out of this miserable mood. I thought I'd make a big effort and be the one to take tea and toast up to Mum. But wouldn't you know it, Ruth had already beaten me to it, had the tray all set out, even a little chrysanthemum in a glass. I gave up.

Madalina was by herself on the bus again. I wondered

whether to sit beside her, but Ruth was behind me and gave me an impatient shove. "Hurry up and sit down! You're blocking the gangway."

So I shared a seat with my sister as usual.

The boys in the back were racketing about as ever, and after a bit Dean appeared and hung over our seat. "Hey!"

"Hey," I replied, my heart sinking. I knew what he wanted this time all right. He'd been sent to arrange a time and a place for a "date" with his mate! Why had I been so stupid as to give him the ghost of an idea I might be interested? I'd have to do some quick thinking and wriggle out of this somehow.

"Russ says . . ." he began, and hesitated. I said impatiently, "Yeah, yeah, just say what you've come to say."

"Well, thing is . . ." he paused again, scratched his head, cleared his throat, and went on, "Thing is, he said to tell you he's changed his mind."

"What?"

"He's changed his mind. Nothing personal, he said to say sorry. He did fancy you. But now he fancies someone else more. Melanie Fisher."

Well! Typical! Talk about girls being fickle! I'd wanted a way out, and this was the perfect one. But I couldn't help feeling miffed, just the same. Melanie Fisher, indeed! I knew her all right, Year Ten, blonde, and very well developed for her age. Some of the boys could hardly take their eyes off her. She could take her pick of them any day. I didn't think a gingery beanstalk like Russell would stand a chance, especially with a pimple on his nose! Catch me feeling sorry for anyone again, and trying to spare their feelings!

Dean cleared off, and Ruth beside me was having a fit of the giggles.

"I think you've been dumped," she said, and doubled up in a fresh wave.

I gave her a dig in the ribs. "Shut it!"

It looked like being another perfect day.

four

As it happened, that Tuesday turned out to be quite interesting, because it was the day the school caught fire.

The alarm went off in the middle of the afternoon, when we were in art class learning about drawing cartoons. I was rather pleased with my drawing of Marge Simpson, and a bit annoyed at the sudden loud interruption. I even had the cheek to ask our art teacher, Miss Charles, if we could just ignore it.

"It's only fire drill. Can't we just carry on with this? Nobody would notice, would they, Miss?"

She gave me a very stern look. "I can't believe you said that, Rachel. You know the drill rules. Everybody out! Now! Pick up your bags but do NOT go to the cloakrooms for anything. Move!"

We moved, with a clatter of feet and chatter of voices, out of the art room and down the stairs to join the other classes streaming out into the car park. It was only then that we noticed a smell of burning, and when we looked at the school building, a cloud of dark smoke was billowing from an upstairs window at the back, where the boys' cloakrooms were. A ripple of excitement ran through the assembled kids. Beechwood High was really on fire!

All around us, people were making stupid comments about what they hoped would happen, and how the fire had started, and a few Year Sevens were panicking and tearful. Our class teacher, Mr Bryce, gathered us together, counting heads. I noticed Madalina, looking absolutely terrified and wanting to join her friends, but we were supposed to stay in our form groups. I went over and put my arm round her. "It's OK. The fire engine'll be here soon, you'll see."

Even as I spoke, two fire engines came hurtling into the school grounds and round the back with a screeching of sirens and flashing of lights. A lot of the kids were desperate to go and watch the action, but were ordered firmly to stay in the car park. Teachers were frantically counting heads and rounding up strays, like anxious sheepdogs. Fire in a school must be one of a teacher's worst nightmares, I thought.

I looked around to check on Ruth, and saw her with the other Year Sevens. None of us had been allowed to go to the cloakrooms for our coats, and it was damp and chilly out of doors, with a bit of drizzle falling.

It was coming up to home time, and the school buses began pulling up. Teachers were shepherding kids onto the buses, making sure that everyone was accounted for. Nobody was allowed back into the building for any reason whatsoever, coats, homework, sports kit, whatever.

My mates all walk home, so I said goodbye to them before getting on our bus. Then a thought struck me. "What about tomorrow?"

"Day off," said Willow. "Mr Bryce just said. It'll be closed."

"How long for?" wondered Chloe.

Willow shook her head. "They'll let us know. Doesn't seem to be much damage, Mr Bryce said, but they have to find out what started the fire, get the electrics checked for faults, that sort of thing."

There was a real sense of tension on the bus, all the local boys hyped up with excitement. Nothing like a touch of disaster to get the adrenalin flowing! The migrant kids were quiet though, looking more apprehensive than anything, keeping their heads well down, talking quietly between themselves. Madalina still looked white and scared, and I had a quick word with Ruth and then sat by Madalina. She was twisting the cuffs of her jumper round and round in her hands.

"Are you OK?"

She looked at me with big frightened eyes. "It scares me."

"The fire? Oh, it wasn't anything much. They're saying some idiot may have set fire to something in the boys' cloakroom. It was soon put out, hardly any damage, they said. They'll check everything over tomorrow." A thought occurred to me. "Have you been in a fire before?"

She shook her head. "It's not that. No, it's not the fire that scares me. It's, it's . . ." She gave a quick motion of her thumb towards the rowdy boys in the back. "It's – it's – them."

I'd hardly noticed what they were going on about, but now I heard one or two remarks among the general din. "Bet it was that Bogdan – he had matches this morning." That was Bryan Davis, a bully and a big-mouth.

"Or Stefan. He's a right weirdo."

"They're all weird – look at 'em! Why don't they stay in their own countries?"

That was Russ Tripp's voice. I looked round at the half-dozen or so Eastern European boys. They were all sitting low in their seats, trying to be invisible, hoodies pulled up or baseball caps pulled down. To be honest, they looked the picture of guilt, but then I've noticed a lot of other boys that age look like that all the time too, shifty and secretive, as though they've just committed some crime. I suppose they get blamed for a lot of stuff and then get into the habit of expecting to be blamed. Vicious circle.

I was getting annoyed with the locals though. Bryan Davis is always a big-mouth, but I was surprised at Russ. To think I'd felt a glimmer of sympathy with him! Boys are like animals when they're in a pack!

The smallest boy, Romanian too, I thought, called Bogdan, began to cry, and the bully-boys picked up on it at once and began to heckle him.

"Aww, little Bogdan, girlie cry-baby! I'd cry too with a name like that!" And they began to chant "Bog – dan! Bog – dan! Bog – dan!"

Madalina gasped beside me. "Bogdan is my cousin! Will they hurt him?"

I felt fury rise inside me. "They certainly will not!" I got to my feet and walked towards the back, fists clenched. "Shut it, you morons! Bunch of idiots! Can you hear yourselves?"

They were surprised and quietened a bit, and one of them said, "ooOOoo!" in that silly way people have. I glared at them all, and one or two of them looked a bit ashamed.

"Bunch of mindless morons!" I said, and then had the feeling I'd said that before. I was still mad as hops but for the life of me couldn't think of anything more original to say to express my contempt. They'd quietened down though, and I'd taken their attention away from the migrant kids. I even saw an admiring look in Russ's eye, and wondered whether he might decide he fancied me more that Melanie Fisher after all. Well, no chance there, matey, after this little episode.

We'd come to our stop and Ruth and I got off. I felt a bit trembly as I climbed down the steps. The boys had got over their surprise and were hooting and making remarks and kissing noises at me. "Bye bye, Rachel! See you tomorrow!"

"Not if I see you first," I said, and then remembered there was no school tomorrow anyway. I saw Madalina's big brown eyes looking at me swimming with tears as the bus door closed, and managed to give her what I hoped was a reassuring smile. My legs were still a bit shaky though as Ruth and I watched the bus depart, the boys still making rude gestures and blowing kisses out of the back window.

Ruth was looking at me with something like admiration.

"You really told them, Rach."

"Somebody had to. Bunch of bullying morons!"

I had the thought again that I'd rather over-used that turn of phrase in the last few minutes, and that I really must get hold of a dictionary and look up some suitably descriptive alternatives, asap, just in case.

five

No school next morning, so that meant a lie-in for Ruth and me. I managed to get in the bathroom first, and went down to the kitchen to find Mum up and about. She looked a bit pale, but smiled brightly as I went into the room.

"Are you feeling better, Mum?"

"Yes, thanks, love. I'm usually fine by about 10. Should be done with this morning sickness in another couple of weeks." She poured a mug of tea and pushed it across the table to me. "Ruth told me about you standing up to those bullies on the bus yesterday. I'm so proud of you. It was a brave thing to do."

I felt faintly embarrassed. Trust Ruth not to be able to keep her mouth shut. Mum paused for a moment, and then said, "Rachel, as you've got the day off, I was thinking . . ." she paused again and took a sip of her own tea. "I have a hospital appointment at 12. A scan. Ted couldn't get time off to come with me, but I was wondering if you'd like to come along, then maybe we could have some lunch and do a bit of shopping." Another pause, another sip of tea. "We haven't done anything like that for ages, just you and me. I've missed it."

I didn't reply for a moment. I'd missed it too, a lot more than I wanted to admit. Mum and I had spent days out together, sometimes, when Ruth was still in primary school. Before she met Ted. Before the Steps came along.

But things were different now. Everything had changed. Even today would revolve around the hospital visit, the scan, the baby. It wasn't really me she wanted, just someone for company. I could hear Ruth in the shower upstairs. Before I could stop myself, I said, "Maybe Ruth would go with you."

She put down her mug and her eyes looked sad. "Ruth's arranged to go round to Helen's for the day. Anyway, I hadn't planned on asking Ruth. It was you I thought I'd like to spend the day with."

Well, I couldn't really think of any good reason not to go. I didn't really fancy it though. Lunch and shopping with Mum, great. Hospital and baby scan, no thanks!

So here I was, sitting not at my school desk but on a shiny black padded seat in the waiting area of the maternity department. It had the usual hospital smell, mostly disinfectant partly disguised by a bunch of lilies on the desk, and the floors were that hard shiny surface they always have that makes your trainers squeak. There were several other pregnant women around, sitting waiting and looking at magazines, or going in and out. All of them looked a lot younger that Mum, some didn't seem all that much older than me. Some of them had enormous bumps that weren't even covered up, one had a pierced belly button on hers with a red sparkly stone, sticking out between her crop top and low-slung sweat pants, like a cherry on a big cup cake.

I wondered how it felt to be pregnant. How Mum felt, with all these much younger expectant mothers around her. How I would feel walking down the street with her when she was the size of a baby elephant. The thought made me inwardly cringe with embarrassment.

I'd expected to have a long boring wait while Mum went in to have the scan, but she and the nurse beckoned me in too. I stayed near the door in the darkened room, while Mum got herself arranged on the couch and the nurses fiddled with the scan equipment. When Mum was lying down with her shirt pulled up I could see that her tummy was not completely flat any more, not a bump exactly but just the hint of a gently convex curve.

The nurses smoothed on gel and faffed about moving this thingy (they said it's called a transducer) over her tummy. The two nurses and Mum were looking at the screen opposite, all agog, and suddenly a nurse said, "There! There it is!" all excited. The other one motioned me to come closer for a better view. I perched on a stool, wondering what I was supposed to see. All it seemed to be was a grainy black and white image with lighter bits, nothing recognisable that I could see.

But the other three were well excited. The nurse pointed out bits to Mum. "See, there's the head. And the tummy. And there's an arm and a leg. He – or she – seems to be sleeping at the moment."

Sleeping? But it's nowhere near being born yet, hardly human, surely!

"Too soon to tell the sex yet," said a nurse. "Next time, maybe. But everything seems to be in order."

I stared hard, wondering how on earth they were making any sense at all of this blurry picture of shapes and shadows.

And then, suddenly, I saw. A large droopy head, with what seemed to be a little blob that might be a nose in profile, a small round tummy, with sprouting little limbs, and on the ends of them, the tiny buds of fingers and toes.

I caught my breath. Mum heard and turned to me, face glowing, and reached out her hand. "Rachel, isn't it wonderful?"

And as we held hands, the little figure on the screen suddenly woke and moved its tiny hand and kicked the leg on the side we could see. The nurses laughed. "See, he or she is waving to you!"

I felt breathless, as though someone had punched me in the stomach. It was a real baby! A living, moving, growing human being, all complete and only needing time to develop. A person! My new little brother or sister. I felt a flicker of excitement, deep inside, and tightened my grip on Mum's hand. Out of nowhere, it seemed, some Bible verses came into my mind that we'd learned by heart at one of Sadie's classes last year. They came back to me, clear as crystal.

"For you created my inmost being; you knit me together in my mother's womb. I praise you because I am fearfully and wonderfully made; your works are wonderful, I know that full well. My frame was not hidden from you when I was made in the secret place. When I was woven together in the depths of the earth, your eyes saw my unformed body. All the days ordained for me were written in your book before one of them came to be."

God had created this new person, in his own image but unique. There would never be another the same. He loved it and had a life all planned out for it. Suddenly I could not wait to see who this new family member would be.

The nurses were chatting to Mum, telling her she'd be able to get a scan photo to take home, with extra copies for a small charge. They were taking away the equipment and Mum was getting herself tidied up.

"I'm dying for the loo," she said. "I had to drink pints of water to make this show up better. Worth it though.

Then we'll have lunch. Chadwick's restaurant? It's a special occasion after all, let's treat ourselves. Then a bit of shopping. Anything you fancy?"

I seemed to be finding it difficult to speak. I nodded. Chadwick's have a fab teen department, and normally I'd jump at the chance to get something from there.

Suddenly, though, that wasn't what I wanted. All of a sudden I remembered that they have a gorgeous mum and baby department as well. With that little figure on the screen still in my mind, I wanted to browse trendy baby-wear, cute little outfits, cuddly toys and blankets. I was going to buy something there, something pretty and soft and special, the nicest present I could get as a first gift from a big sister to welcome her new baby sister or brother.

PART TWO
Annie's Story

LETTING GO

one

That week wasn't exactly an ordinary one, even not counting the little matter of the school catching fire. All kinds of other things were going on. For a start, I thought I'd sussed out what to do about our family situation.

Ever since we'd moved here, life had been a kind of see-saw experience for me. Big highs and deep lows. More of the lows, to begin with. I'd been bullied at my old school and was scared of being bullied again. I'd thought the main reason for us moving was for me to have a fresh start at a new school.

Wrong. Or at least, only partly right. The main reason was that my parents were splitting up.

I didn't believe it when Mum first broke the news to me and my little brother Harry. "Divorcing?" I asked incredulously. She nodded and I stared at her in horror. "You can't be! You can't, Mum!"

My brother was crying and saying that he wanted Dad. Mum looked white and drawn. I babbled on, "You can go to counselling or something, Mum, you can sort it out. Can't you? You've got to!"

But she shook her head. "No, love. He's left. For good."

Splitting is an apt word, kind of hard and sharp,

rending and tearing. I looked it up in the dictionary; some of the definitions are: "to break, to cleave, to divide, to go to pieces". That's just how it was. Our lives split. My family split, broken and divided. All of us going to pieces.

That's how it felt. The strange thing is, although you think things will never be right again, never be normal, you seem to adjust. Harry seemed to be almost back to normal very soon, going to school and playing with his mates. Mum looked sad but liked her new job and the new house and made some friends at work. Dad spoke to all of us on the phone, and was planning regular visits.

I was angry. How dare he walk away like that! Oh, I know he still provided well for us all, he wasn't like some men who go off and leave their families without a penny. Dad has a good job, and we certainly weren't left on the breadline. I suppose we could even have managed without Mum working at all, but as she said, why would she want to sit at home all day brooding about why and how things went wrong? As it was, we had got into a routine of sorts.

All the same, if Dad thought we'd go on just as usual, he could think again. He phoned after a couple of weeks wanting to see me and Harry.

"I'm not going!" I said indignantly when Mum told me they'd set up a meeting.

She looked at me wearily. "Oh, go on, please, love. You need to keep in touch and he'll probably take you for a nice meal or something."

"He can take Harry," I said stubbornly. "I'm not going."

And I didn't. He and Harry went to McDonalds and Harry came home pleased as punch because he'd had a Happy Meal (!) with a stupid walking plastic dinosaur in it. Dad had bought him new trainers with flashing lights on them too, which annoyed Mum no end, because he'd only just got new ones, and you can't put the ones with lights on in the washing machine when they're grubby. And these would soon get grubby, because they were white. Typical! Just like Dad not to think of something like that.

He'd bought me a present too, a pink rucksack with sparkly bits, the kind of thing I'd have liked when I was about five years old.

"It's the thought that counts, love," said Mum, who seemed determined to be fair to Dad no matter what he'd done. Inside the bag was a matching purse, and inside that a whole roll of £10 and £20 notes. I looked at the wad of money in my hand, not even bothering to count it. Did he think he could buy himself back into our good books? Harry'd been given money too, which Mum took and put safely away.

I shoved the rucksack and purse into the back of the wardrobe and the money in my top drawer. Maybe I'd spend it, maybe not. Either way, I didn't want to see my dad.

Those were the low points, but there'd been high ones too. Like making new friends – in particular, Willow, Rachel, Holly, Chloe and Amber. They're a great bunch, though I thought them a little weird to begin with. They all go to this club in town, the Beech Bank Club, a kind of Christian youth thing run by the vicar and his wife. I don't normally go much for youth clubs, the ones I'd been to before all had little exclusive cliques and I didn't seem to fit in with any. I fitted in fine at BB though. Nobody is allowed to be mean or to ignore other people, and if they have differences they have to be sorted out. Bitchiness is frowned on, there's no alcohol, drugs or smoking allowed, and pairing off is not encouraged.

Put like that, it all sounds kind of restrictive and regimented, but it isn't at all really. I like the safe kind of feeling there, like, whoever you are, whatever your faults, you'll be accepted. And there's no way it's dull and boring. Anything but!

One thing I did find strange was the way the girls talked about praying. Like, whenever one of them had some problem, or hassle with someone, or anything bothering them, they'd say, "Let's pray about it." And not just when they went to church, or the BB club. They'd do it anywhere, anytime. Even in school. They'd been allowed to use a special little room once a week as a prayer room.

"But don't you have to be in a proper church to pray?" I asked Willow one day, when they were heading for the room. "I mean, can anyone do it? I thought it had to be a proper vicar, or priest, and saying the proper words."

She shook her head of flaming red hair. "No, anyone can. It used to be just priests in the olden days. But since

Jesus died, everybody is free to pray to God whenever they want and wherever they happen to be."

This puzzled me. Willow said she'd explain more to me when there was time, maybe with Sadie at Beech Bank. They all talked a lot about Jesus. I was even more puzzled because, from R.E. lessons at my old school, I thought he was a historical character who'd lived a long time ago and been crucified.

"Isn't that true then?" I asked, when I'd been to BB a few times. We were sitting over a coffee, waiting for Rachel and Amber, who'd been shooting pool with some of the boys in the games room. Sadie was sitting with us, feet up on a spare chair, hugging a coffee mug. She and Willow had been discussing the Enquirers' class – apparently one of the girls had asked the same question as mine. Both she and Willow turned to look at me and I felt my face flame with embarrassment.

"Yes, it is true, of course," she said slowly, putting down her mug. "But there's more to it than that."

And she explained to me that Jesus had truly been crucified, he'd been dead and buried, but that God had raised him to life again. That because of this, because he took all the sin of humankind on himself when he died, everyone can be forgiven their sins. That Jesus lives by faith in everyone that receives him into their heart and life. That he will be our friend, our helper, the one we can pray to at any time, who will never leave us, fail us or let us down. That we are all precious to him and that he loves us more than anyone else will ever love us.

I didn't really understand most of what she said.

Sadie said she'd find some helpful leaflets that might make things clearer. My thoughts were spinning as I went home. My mind was telling me this was all made-up stuff, that none of it could really be proved. It wasn't rational. Wasn't it Karl Marx who said that religion is the opiate of the masses, or something like that? How could these claims about Jesus be proved?

And yet – there was something about him that drew me. I wanted to learn more. I wanted that extra something that Sadie and Rod and the other girls had. I knew it was something to do with Jesus. Almost like a friendship with him, if that was possible with someone you couldn't hear, see, touch, and who you weren't quite sure existed anyway!

My mind was going in circles. I didn't know what to think. But that night, for the first time since I was little, I knelt down by my bed and prayed:

"Jesus, I don't know if you're real or if you can hear me. But if you are, and you can, I want to know you like the others do. I want you to be in my life. I want you to help me."

And I added "Amen" because I thought that was the right thing to do.

two

I didn't feel any different after that prayer – at least, not at first. But I found myself thinking about

Jesus more and more, drinking in all I heard about him at Beech Bank. I'd even been to church once or twice.

The afternoon of the school fire, Willow and I walked home together. We live quite close to each other, and she has a young brother called Rowan who's palled up with Harry. We're in and out of each other's houses quite a lot.

"Do you want to come in for a bit?" asked Willow as we reached her road. "No school tomorrow, so no rush on homework – yay!"

We'd been discussing the fire all the way home, like all the rest of the groups of kids going home from Beechwood High. Everyone was twittering with excitement. I'd heard the opinion several times that the migrant kids were somehow behind it. Willow thought that was a stupid idea.

"Why on earth would they want to set the school on fire?"

"Maybe they don't like school here. They do get picked on a lot."

"So they solve it by burning the school down? A bit drastic! I don't think so." She paused. "If you noticed, the ones kicking off with that idea are the same ones who pick on the kids most. Another excuse for future bullying, maybe?"

That hadn't occurred to me. But Willow has a "wise head on her shoulders", as I'd heard one teacher once remark to another. She seems older than the rest of us somehow, though she's the same age.

Both of us were chilly by the time we reached Willow's house, as our jackets were still in the school cloakroom, and I was glad to accept her invitation. We made ourselves mugs of coffee and carried them upstairs to Willow's bedroom. Willow's house is . . . interesting. Her parents are laid-back – her mum's an artist – and most of the house is usually in a bit of a muddle. But going into Willow's room is like stepping into another world. She's decorated it herself, all cool blues and silvery metal and keeps it absolutely pristine. She has beautiful clothes, all paid for with her own hard-earned money, and when her wardrobe doors are open it's like being in some cool boutique.

We kicked off our shoes and she flopped down on the bed while I took the pale blue suede beanbag, being mega-careful with my coffee – a spill would spell disaster.

We were still talking about the fire and the migrant kids. Willow thought we should be doing more to help them. Then my mobile rang. I jumped, and had a near miss with my coffee. I put the mug down carefully on a clear plastic mat before answering and was glad I had, because I felt my hands begin to tremble as I recognised the voice. It was my dad.

"Annie? How are you, sweetheart? I thought I'd catch you for a chat before the others get home. Harry's at after-school club, isn't he?"

He sounded slightly anxious, unsure of my reaction. I'd hardly exchanged half a dozen words with him since he left. I said, through lips that suddenly felt tight and stiff, "Yes, he is. I'm fine, thank you."

A pause. Was he waiting for me to ask him how he was too? Well, I wasn't going to. He cleared his throat, and went on, "Thing is, I've missed you, Annie. A lot. I know things are – difficult – just now, but it would be good to talk. I have a few days off work this week. I was wondering if we could get together, just you and me. Old Harry does jabber on a bit, doesn't he? I'll see him as well, another time, of course. But I wondered if you and I could meet one afternoon this week, after school or something?"

He sounded almost pleading. My throat ached, and my mouth felt dry. I managed to say, stiffly, "I don't think I'll be able to. I've got – things to do – all this week." And then I couldn't seem to speak any more, so I ended up in a rush, "Sorry Dad, got to go. I'm not at home, I'm at my friend's. Bye."

As I fumbled to switch off, I heard him say, sadly, "Well, give me a ring if you change your mind. You have my number."

I sat there choking back the tears. Willow had got off the bed and wandered over to her desk to switch on the computer, checking her mail to give me some space and privacy. She twirled round on the chair to face me. "You OK, Annie?"

I tried to nod, but it didn't work. You can't hope to fool Willow anyway. I dropped my head into my heads and burst into tears.

Willow jumped up and came over and squeezed onto

the beanbag with me, putting her arms round me and holding me tight. I sobbed and sobbed, until there was a big wet patch on the front of Willow's school top. She pressed a tissue into my hands and then got up and passed me the whole box. I mopped my face, feeling completely wrung out.

"You really miss your dad, don't you?"

I nodded and blew my nose. She'd hit the nail right on the head. I put on this act of being mad at my dad and not wanting to see him, but really I miss him so badly that it hurts. I want him to come home, and for things to be as they were before, the four of us all together. I just want him to come back.

I felt I was about to start all over again, so I blew my nose again, cleared my throat and tried to pull myself together. Willow was sitting cross-legged on the carpet at my feet, looking at me thoughtfully. "You know, we should be doing something about it."

"What do you mean? What *can* we do?"

"Pray."

Should have guessed. But I didn't see how it could make any difference. They were getting divorced, for goodness' sake! I must have looked doubtful, because Willow said, "Prayer can change things. There's a verse in the Bible that says . . ."

She grabbed her Bible from the bedside table and leafed through it for the verse, found it, and read it out . . . "*Therefore I tell you, whatever you ask for in prayer, believe that you have received it, and it will be yours.*"

"Do you think that really happens?" I asked rather dubiously.

"'Course." And she turned over more pages and found another verse.

"If two of you on earth agree about anything you ask for, it will be done for you by my Father in heaven."

I still had my doubts. We couldn't really pray that Dad would come back, could we? It seemed more than I could dare to hope for. But Willow knew far more about such things, didn't she?

"Let's do it," she said.

"Right now?"

"Yeah, why not?" She wriggled to a more comfortable position, and began "Dear Father God, we . . ." But then there was a loud slam of a door downstairs, and voices in the hallway. "Willow? Are you back? Is it true there was a fire in school?" called her mum's voice.

"Drat!" said Willow. "Mum and Rowan. No peace now, they'll be busting in here any minute." She called out, "Yes Mum, tell you all about it in a minute," and then turned back to me. "Tell you what, give me a ring later and we'll pray on the phone."

"Can you do that?"

"'Course. You can pray anywhere you can talk. You don't need to talk, even. You can do it quietly in your mind."

Well, as I said, she knows more than me on the subject, so that is what we did later that same evening. Mostly it was she who did the praying, out loud, because I didn't quite know how to put things, but I agreed with everything she said. And later still, when I was going to bed, I knelt down and prayed my own prayer.

"God, Willow says that you can do impossible things, because it says so in your book. So I'm asking you to do an impossible thing and bring my dad back and make our family like it was before. Thank you for listening. Amen."

three

Next morning I woke up feeling different. Lighter somehow, and free, as though some heavy weight had lifted off me. It took me a minute or two to remember the prayer I'd prayed.

It was quiet in the house, Harry having gone off to school as usual and Mum to work. I padded round in my pjs and bare feet, eating cereal and wondering about how prayer works. I mean, how on earth does God manage to hear every single person who prays to him, probably all at the same time, and then work out what to do about them all? Then the phone rang.

"Annie?" said Amber's voice. "Are you up?" I said I was, through a mouthful of cornflakes. "Well," she said "I'm ringing round to see if the girls want to come out on a hike with me and Hamlet. It's such a fantastic day."

It was, too. Sun was streaming through the windows, a breeze fluttering the autumn leaves on the apple tree in our garden. Perfect day for getting out and about, even with Hamlet in attendance. Hamlet is Amber's puppy, nice enough but excitable and inclined to yap at every cat, dog and moving object he sees. Yet for some reason I hesitated. Amber was rattling on, "Rach can't come, she's going somewhere with her mum, but I'm meeting Chloe and Willow in about an hour. We might go along the river footpath and then up into the farmland."

It sounded perfect, and I really wanted to go. But there was something I wanted more, and I heard myself saying, "Really sorry, Ams, love to go but I'm doing something else. Seeing my dad, actually."

She sounded disappointed and a bit surprised, but she said she hoped I'd have a good time. I hung up, very surprised at myself. All of a sudden, I really, really wanted to see my dad. God must have changed me too. He was really doing something. My heart gave a little skip of excitement.

My dad sounded the most surprised of all when I called him, as well he might, seeing how crabby I'd been the day before. A slight pause, then he said, "Well, that's great! Yes, yes, of course we can meet. It's a very good idea, in fact. There's something I really want to discuss with you. Lunch at Chadwick's? I'll book a table. Shall I come out and pick you up?"

For some reason, I said no, I'd get the bus. For one thing, Dad lives 20 miles or so the other side of the city, and it would mean a lot of extra driving for him. Also I think I had some idea of swanning into Chadwick's

posh restaurant, all glammed up, and meeting my
dad like some scene from a film. I'm getting to be a
worse drama queen than Amber! I spent ages faffing
about deciding what to wear, and all the time I was
thinking, "He's coming home! He's coming back to
us! That must be what he wants to discuss!" And I
was totally gobsmacked, awed and overwhelmed at the
awesome way God was already answering my prayers
and Willow's!

In the end I hit on a stripy mini-dress, black tights,
my new boots and a black denim jacket with silver
studs. I washed and blow-dried my hair, and brushed it
till it shone like silk. I had to admit it, I looked good. I
wouldn't let Dad down, posh restaurant or not.

I got the bus into the city, 35 minutes ride away.
I was early, and hung around for a bit in the High
Street, not wanting to seem over eager. Then I went to
Chadwick's.

Chadwick's is like another world, discreet and
elegant, each department beautifully arranged (and
frighteningly expensive). No pushing and shoving
and scrabbling for bargains here! Soft music playing,
deep carpets underfoot, immaculate assistants with
long manicured nails and snooty expressions. I
wondered how people still managed to shop here with
the recession and everything, but evidently they did. I
got into the lift and sailed up to the restaurant on the
top floor.

The restaurant was only half full, just a soft murmur
of conversation from the lunchers and the discreet

clink of cutlery on china. Everyone terribly well-heeled and well-dressed, that is, except for two people at a table by the window who stuck out like sore thumbs. Rachel and her mum! Both of them wore jeans, hoodies and trainers, but neither was giving a hoot. They were eating gooey desserts in tall glasses and giggling like idiots, having a great time. They didn't even see me and I didn't go over. I was looking for my dad.

And there he was, at one of the tables to the side of the room. He looked a bit older, I thought, a bit anxious, but then he saw me and his face broke into a big smile.

"Annie! You made it! Lovely to see you!"

I went over, heart thudding. He stood up and gave me a big hug, and I smelled the familiar smell of his soap and after-shave. "I thought you might change your mind again. There's such a lot to talk about. Sit down. I'll get you a drink."

I began to slide into the seat opposite, but suddenly froze in my tracks and my blood ran cold. Two things happened at exactly the same time. I saw that the table was set for three, not two. And at the very same moment, I noticed that a young woman was approaching from the cloakroom direction, heading for our table. She was a girl, really, maybe still in her twenties, pretty, dark-haired and slim. She smiled uncertainly in my direction, and Dad cleared his throat and said nervously, "Annie, I'd like you to meet Samantha. Sam, this is my lovely daughter, Annie."

And the scales fell from my eyes, and I realised what

a fool I'd been. Dad wasn't planning on coming back at all. He had a girlfriend! This – this Samantha, in a cream trouser suit, years younger than Mum, probably the reason he left in the first place! Dad had brought me here on purpose to meet her! I couldn't believe that he could be so heartless, so cruel!

Tears blurred my eyes and I scrambled to my feet, jarring the table and grabbing my bag. Dad was saying, "Annie? Please sit down. Let's have some lunch and talk . . ."

No way! I was getting out of there fast and I never wanted to see him again. Neither of them. Through eyes swimming with tears I saw their faces, disappointed and dismayed, upset and anxious and pleading. The girl, Samantha, said uncertainly, "I did wonder whether this was a good idea."

I ignored her. I said shakily, "Goodbye Dad," and stumbled blindly towards the cloakroom area.

On the way I lurched against another table and some cutlery fell to the floor, and I heard a woman tut-tutting and saying something about drugs. Rachel and her mum had seen me now and I heard Rach's voice say enquiringly, "Annie?" but I took no notice. In the ladies, I dived into the furthest cubicle, locked the door, sat on the toilet seat and sobbed and sobbed. How could Dad do this? He'd never come back now that he had another woman.

After a while I heard someone come into the cloak-room. I held my breath. Surely, surely, that Samantha wouldn't have had the nerve to come in after me.

Then I heard Rachel's voice. "Annie? Annie, are you in there? Annie, open the door!"

I didn't answer for a moment. But she persisted, and I knew she wouldn't go away. Rachel is like a stubborn little bulldog when she wants to be. Besides, I needed her so badly. I opened the door and fell into her arms.

Rachel ran the cold tap and mopped me up with loads of Chadwick's pale lilac quilted paper towels, murmuring soothing things. I blurted out my story between gulps and sobs. She listened with great sympathy, patting me and clucking like a mother hen. "That's unbelievable! So totally mega tactless of him! But that's men for you. No imagination at all."

I supposed it had been just thoughtlessness on Dad's part, presenting the situation in the way he had. But the cold facts remained. He had a girlfriend and would therefore not be returning to us.

"Would you like to come to mine?" asked Rachel. I shook my head. Her mum and Ruth would be there, and I couldn't face anyone just yet.

"Shall we run you home then?" she asked, but I shook my head again. "No, I'll get the bus back. I need to think. Do me a favour, Rach. Go out and see if the coast's clear. I can't face seeing Dad and that woman again if they're still there."

I escaped and got the next bus, riding home with my hot cheek pressed against the window and my stomach rumbling for lack of lunch. It had been a total fiasco. I'd believed God was answering prayer and it had been one big sick joke. Things were even worse than before. Hadn't God heard me, or didn't he care?

Back home, I flung myself on the bed and sobbed again.

"God, why has this happened? I trusted you and you let me down. I don't know if I can ever believe in you again. I just don't understand. Why did it happen like this? Why? Why?"

four

Of course, I had to tell Mum what had happened. I couldn't stall her enquiries about the lunch for long, and anyway, I knew my swollen eyelids and blotchy face would tell their own story. So I told it just as it was, that evening in the kitchen when Harry was upstairs on the playstation.

To my surprise, Mum wasn't devastated as I'd feared. Quite philosophical about the whole thing, in fact. She tut-tutted a bit about the insensitive way Dad had sprung Samantha on me, and sympathised with my upset feelings, but said that's just the way Dad is, he's never been a sensitive person and goodness knows it's no use thinking he'll change now.

And she knew all about Samantha! It seemed that Samantha had nothing to do with the marriage break-up, she and Dad had only met since the split. It had been love at first sight, apparently. Mum thought it might not last, it might be just Dad being flattered by the attentions of a younger woman. If it fizzled out, well and good, if not, well, we just had to get on with our lives.

I was amazed by her attitude. "But don't you *mind*, Mum?"

She looked sad then, but pulled a face and said, quite quietly, "Of course the end of a marriage is always sad. But I came to terms with the heartache a long time ago. We haven't been getting along for some time, you know. Kind of drifted apart, I suppose. Fell out of love."

I'd never known any of that. Mum looked at me, and said, "We tried to keep going for you and Harry. The move here was to have been one final go at a fresh start. It didn't work out. We both knew it. We're happier apart, if the truth be told. And I hope we can all stay on amicable terms."

I didn't know what to say or think. The structure of my world seemed to be falling apart, brick by brick. I'd been sure that God was going to put our family back together. And now it all seemed hopeless.

Mum reached across the table and patted my hand. "Try and forgive us, love. Or at least accept. Don't shut your dad out. He's still your dad, and he does love you."

Strangely, I could believe that, remembering the anguished look in his eyes when I'd jumped up from the table. I went to bed slightly comforted, but only slightly.

"Oh, by the way," said Mum as I headed for the stairs.

"The school rang and it's closed for another day. Open again Friday."

I slept badly, and when Rachel rang next morning to see how I was, I was still in bed. She said the others were getting together to talk about something at Willow's that afternoon, and did I want to come? I said no thanks, that I was having a very quiet day. And I hoped it wasn't me that they were talking about. Rachel assured me she hadn't breathed a word, and to have a nice day, and that they'd call round for me later on the way to Beech Bank.

I soon wished I'd gone round to Willow's with the others. It was dull on my own at home, lounging about watching boring daytime TV and doing silly games and quizzes on the Internet. I wondered what they were talking about and planning. Maybe they'd tell me later this afternoon.

Earlier, I'd seriously debated not going to BB any more. It was all centred on God, and I wasn't sure I believed in him any more since yesterday. He was supposed to be very strong on marriage and families, yet he was letting ours fall apart and not caring at all. Maybe the whole God-thing was just one big fairy tale.

But by mid-afternoon I was so bored with my own company that I got out of my pjs, showered and dressed, and was very glad to see the others when they turned up on my doorstep. Willow, Chloe and Amber seemed high as kites on the hike they'd had out into the country yesterday, which had been quite adventurous as it turned out. They promised they'd fill me in on the details later. Rachel hadn't breathed a word to them about my lunch fiasco, for which I was grateful. She was wittering on about the wonderful time she'd had at the hospital with her mum, seeing the new baby on a scan. Well, each to their taste, I suppose. It didn't sound like my idea of fun.

It was quieter than usual at Beech Bank, Beechwood High being closed. A lot of the kids go straight there after school, some do homework in the quiet area or play pool or table tennis. Quite a few had turned up though all the same, it's the kind of place you want to hang out in, school or no school. Sadie was there, getting the big room ready for tomorrow night's big event, whatever that might turn out to be. We helped her set out chairs. Rod was checking the sound system.

"Is it a gig?" asked Amber.

Sadie smiled and tapped her nose. "Wait and see."

"Why won't you tell us?" asked Willow. "I mean, usually when there's something special, we have posters up and flyers and invitations and all that."

Sadie smiled again. "Reason One, it was arranged at very short notice so no time for all that. Reason Two, a bit of reverse psychology. If you're all kept guessing, you're more likely to turn up."

She's not daft, is Sadie. She can see as far through a brick wall as anybody. I noticed her giving me a keen look or two, and a little later she got me by myself. "Something's bothering you, isn't it, Annie?"

I sighed. But I wanted to get it all off my chest. Sadie beckoned me into the snug, which is where we go to be private. I told her everything, about our family situation, my feelings about my dad, my prayers with Willow and the bitter disappointment.

She listened carefully, elbow on the table and chin resting on her hand. When I'd finished, she didn't speak for a moment. I felt I had to justify my conclusions, and said, "I just don't understand. God is supposed to want families to stay together, right? I mean, you and Rod always say that in your talks, that marriage is a lifelong commitment, that children need two parents."

She thought again, and then said, "Yes, that's all true, and that's God's ideal plan for us. But we're living in a world that's less than ideal, a pretty sick one, in fact. Marriages do go wrong, and sadly, they can't always be mended."

"Mum said they'd fallen out of love," I said forlornly.

"Yes, well, it does happen. To most couples, I'd say. Christian ones too. But the thing is, if you're committed to making it work, the chances are you'll fall in love again. With the same person."

This was a new idea to me. But it didn't help in our case. "Not much chance of that now. He's in love with Samantha."

"Yes. Well, we just have to leave it all in God's hands. There's a verse in the Bible that says his ways are not our ways, and that his ways are far better than ours."

"But Willow said that if we prayed, God would sort it out. She said he can do things that really seem impossible."

"Yes, and that's true too. But all kinds of other things

are involved too. As humans we all have free will. We're all free to choose. And sometimes we make wrong choices and have to live with them. We just have to accept the consequences of our own actions and the actions of others."

"That's what Mum said."

Sadie nodded. "I'm sure she's right. Just keep praying for your dad, and all your family. God might not bring him back, but he'll answer prayer in ways you've never dreamed of."

"But I want him back!"

I felt a sob rise in my throat. Sadie reached out and squeezed my hand in both of hers. "I know, sweetie. But don't ever forget just how much God loves you. You're so precious to him, and he's the Father who's always there."

"But I don't think I can believe that any more!"

"Never mind! It doesn't make any difference. He still loves you just the same. He won't leave you, and he doesn't mind if you're angry. Try not to judge your dad too harshly. Things will change, you'll see."

I think she prayed a little prayer, but I really can't remember what she said. I do remember the big hug she gave me though, and the way she kept her arm around my shoulders when we went to join the others. They were sweet too, not asking nosey questions but just being there. I was so glad I'd gone to BB, and I went home comforted.

I'd decided prayer was a total waste of time. But when I went to bed, I found myself saying, out loud,

"Maybe you're real after all, God, because Sadie and Rod and the others all believe in you. And they're different from other people, and it's because of you. So maybe, just maybe, I won't give up on you yet."

five

Back at school next day, there really wasn't much to show there'd been a fire at all, except for a lingering smell of burnt rubber around the boys' cloakroom area. Many of us thought it was an improvement on the usual pong that hung about there, of sweaty games kit and bad feet, as though half of them had athlete's foot (which they probably had). It had been discovered that the cause of the blaze had been a collection of trainers on the floor of the changing rooms, piled up and set alight.

Why somebody would want to do that was anyone's guess. The migrant children were still being blamed, very illogically, we thought. Half of them hadn't turned up at school today, and somehow that was considered proof of their guilt. Those of us with a brain could work out that it was because they were scared stiff of repercussions. But there seemed to be a group of lads in Year Ten who had no brain at all, and were all too keen to go along with potential bullies like Bryan Davis and Kyle Lennox, whose mentality was positively Neanderthal. "Although that's an insult to the Neanderthals," said Rachel, who has to travel on the bus with some of them.

Madalina was there though, and the others had decided that we must make a real effort to be friends with her, as we'd found she was the only migrant girl in school. So Rachel made a point of nabbing her at the end of the last period before lunch and asking her to sit with us.

She seemed very dubious, looking nervously around for the other migrant kids. But none of the other Romanians seemed to be in sight, and she came with us to our table. Madalina seemed to trust Rachel, though she still acted very shy and kept her head well down. She'd got different clothes from somewhere in an attempt to blend in. The migrants are not required to wear school uniform, as they're here for so short a time. The boys wear jeans and hoodies mostly. Some of them used to wear very strange big floppy caps, but they've wised up and got baseball caps instead. Madalina though had been coming to school in a long droopy kind of skirt and jumper which made her stick out like a sore thumb. Today she was wearing jeans, sweatshirt and trainers, all brand new but very cheap-looking, the jeans not quite the right fit or in-style, the trainers the kind that fall to bits after the first machine wash. I felt a stab of pity for her, remembering my own first day here, when I hadn't had uniform either. Although my clothes had been good quality ones.

We all sat round a table for six with our plates of

macaroni cheese and salad. I guessed Madalina got free dinners.

"How are you liking school, Madalina?" asked Willow, in an attempt to get a conversation going.

Madalina looked at Willow with big brown eyes. She gulped down a mouthful of macaroni cheese and said, "Thank you, yes, I like school very much. School is good."

I was surprised, both by the way she was quickly learning English, and by the fact that she liked school.

"Did you go to school in Romania?"

She nodded, but then said, "Yes, but not all the time. Not often." She hesitated, looked round at our faces, and went on, "In my country, my people do not go to school too much."

"Aren't there schools in Romania then? I didn't know that."

Madalina hesitated again before answering. I thought how difficult it must be to carry on a conversation in a language not your own. I didn't think I'd be able to do it in French or Spanish, which I'd been taking for over three years.

Then she said, "Yes, there are schools. But not for everyone. Not everyone is welcome. Not for us. You see, we . . . we are Roma."

Most of us stared at her, not quite understanding, and Amber said, "Roma? Is that different to Romanian?"

Chloe twigged right away though. "Oh yes, I saw a TV programme about Roma. They're travellers, aren't they? Gypsies?" I heard Amber give a little gasp and she and Chloe looked at each other.

Madalina's head went up, and the scared look was replaced by one of defiant pride. "Yes, I am Roma. Gypsy, as they say. But proud to be. But – others – treat us badly."

"Even in your own country?"

"There, especially. We are treated like outcasts. Like not really people, even though our music and dancing is better than theirs! Not all schools will take Roma children. So we teach ourselves. But that is hard. Very hard."

Now that she had begun to talk, Madalina didn't seem to want to stop. She laid down her fork and said, "That is why I come here. To learn, to go to school. Even for a short time. My uncle has taught me English. When he says he is bringing his family here for the potato harvest, I beg and plead to go with them. My family don't like to let me go. They think I will be in danger, but I cry and plead and they let me go. I work hard. I learn quick. It is very good, except . . ."

"Except for those idiots who think it's fun to torment anyone who's different," finished Rachel.

Madalina nodded. "I did not think it would be like that here. They said Britain is not a nation that discriminates."

I think we all felt a bit ashamed. Chloe leaned over and gave Madalina's hand a squeeze. "We're so sorry. But please try and trust us. We'll be your friends, right, girls?"

There was a chorus of assent all round the table. Madalina's eyes were swimming with tears now. She bent her head over her plate and whispered, "Thank you."

Going back to class that afternoon I felt both humbled and indignant on Madalina's behalf. How fortunate my life had been, despite its ups and downs. And how terrible that a girl of my own age could live with discrimination and the fear of hatred hanging over her head.

Later that afternoon, another incident happened that made my indignation rise to a fresh level. Coming out of school, I noticed a group of boys hanging around the back of the bus stop. School hours were over, and nobody was taking much notice in the rush to get home. But I saw that there was someone there in the middle of them, and a brief glimpse between the shifting bodies showed me that it was one of the migrant boys. Most of them, including Madalina, had got on the bus with Rachel and the bus was ready to leave.

Without even stopping to think, I rushed over. One or two lads were holding on to a small Year Seven boy, I think it was the one called Bogdan, stopping him from getting the bus home. He was crying, completely helpless while they laughed like drains. I shuddered to think what might happen to him if he got stranded here in town all on his own.

I'd been bullied myself at my old school, and knew the feeling exactly. There'd been no one to help me then. Nobody seemed to be bothering about this boy.

And I was scared. Normally I avoided hassle like the plague. I sent up a quick prayer, forgetting that I wasn't really sure I believed in God any more. "Help me, God! Please help me!"

And I heard my own voice say, "Stop that right now! Let him go!"

A couple of the big boys laughed and sneered. "Listen to her!" I'd surprised them though. Surprised myself even more. I shoved my way between them and grabbed the scared little boy by the arm. "Let go, I said!"

"He's only a snotty little foreigner," said one. "Shouldn't be here at all."

But they loosened their grip. I dragged the little boy out from among them and ran him to the bus, shoving him through the doors just as it was revving the engine ready to go.

It had all happened almost in a split second. The other girls were staring at me open-mouthed. I felt my cheeks burning and my heart was racing. "Wow, Annie," said Willow admiringly. "That was quick thinking. Good on ya!"

"It wasn't anything," I mumbled. I couldn't believe I'd really done it, myself, and I didn't want to talk about it. Willow soon twigged how I was feeling, and after we'd said goodbye to Chloe and Amber, we mostly talked about what we were going to wear that evening for BB. We reckoned we'd better pull out all the stops, you never knew what might be on the agenda.

I felt that my eyes had been opened that day, big time, and thought about it while I was in the shower.

So much hatred and injustice in the world, so much hardship and ignorance and intolerance, right here on our own doorstep. And I was suddenly ashamed all over again, remembering my own refusal to try and understand my own dad, who I loved and who loved me, whatever else had happened.

I laid out my clothes on the bed, leggings and a floaty short dress. And then I texted my dad and said I was sorry about yesterday, and that I'd like to go along when he took Harry out at the weekend.

And then I prayed.

"God, I'm sorry for the mean way I act and think sometimes. Thank you for helping me today. I'm sorry I was mad at you. Please help me to love you more, and to love other people. And thank you for loving us all."

PART THREE

Chloe's Story

GETTING STARTED

one

Things have changed quite a bit at our house. Mostly for the better, I have to say. For one thing, Peter is a different person. The depression he had since the serious road accident and its repercussions has gone, and Dad and I have the old Peter back. He's back at school, playing sport and enjoying life, and a big black cloud has lifted from us all.

Then there's Auntie Sue. I'd lived with Auntie Sue for a while after my mum died (I was not even four then) until I got so homesick that they brought me home. Auntie Sue has always been there in the background. Now, all of a sudden, she's right there in the foreground, so to speak. In our house, in fact. Living with us.

Auntie Sue is Dad's older sister. Quite a bit older, as it happens. She's a widow now, she retired early from teaching, her only son lives in Dubai and I suppose she was a bit lonely. Anyway, she decided she'd like to be nearer to us, and that she'd sell her house in Hampshire and buy a smaller one in our area. Dad invited her to stay with us while she was looking. So she's here. If you ask me, it's going to be permanent.

I'm very fond of Auntie Sue, and I must say there are lots of advantages to her being here. It is fantastic having a nice cooked meal to come home to and not having to get takeaways or poke about in the freezer looking for something quick and easy to microwave. It is nice to have the washing and ironing done and the house cleaned. Nice to have the odd chat when I feel the need. If only it stopped there.

But it doesn't. Aunt Sue has taken over. Made me and Peter (and Dad too, but he hasn't twigged it's happening yet) her Mission in Life. Which often comes close to interference. Very close.

For example, our diet has changed. Auntie Sue threw up her hands in horror when she found that our breakfasts were mostly a cup of tea and bowl of Honey Krunchies on the run.

"That is quite wrong. Too much sugar will produce an initial burst of energy which will soon burn out and leave you depleted. You need slow-release food to get you through the morning."

So she has us on high-protein breakfasts; eggs, or grilled bacon, or something called kedgeree, a mixture of cooked fish, hard-boiled egg and rice all chopped up together, which sounds gross but is actually quite nice. We have five portions of fruit and veg per day, minimum, and she checks to make sure. We eat organic dairy foods, and meat with the British kite mark, which Peter pointed out is not always British produced but just tested in the UK. We support local farmers whenever possible, to ensure freshness. Food shopping takes three times as long as it used to, because we have to scrutinise every label for fat content and hidden sugar, and additives with an E. Quick fixes from the chippy or the Chinese are mostly a fond memory.

And it's not only the food. Aunt Sue has taken my wardrobe in hand, which means tut-tutting at the length of my skirts (minis are just above the knee, according to her), the tightness of my jeans (very conducive to certain infections), skimpiness of underwear and general lack of winter insulation. She has it on reliable report that crop tops in cold weather have resulted in an epidemic of kidney trouble in young girls.

"I'm going shopping for warm tights and underwear for the winter," she announced a couple of weeks ago. "Could I see what vests you have, please?"

Mystified, I showed her my vest tops; a pink, a purple, an orange, a grey marl and a black one with silver sequins on the straps that I save for edgy evening events (Not too frequent, those). She tut-tutted some more. "No, no, I don't mean those skimpy things. I mean proper warm winter vests, preferably wool mix, winter underwear, you know."

I gazed at her in horror. She couldn't possibly want me to wear those things, all the time, under school blouses and all? I'd be the laughing stock of the girls' changing room! That's what she did mean, though. I comforted myself with the thought that vests like that hadn't been manufactured for the last forty years at least, and she'd never find any. But Auntie Sue tracked down the last existing ones and carried them home in triumph. Cream coloured, with picot edging, little satin bows and built-up shoulders. Not even shoulder straps!

So far I've got by by stuffing them under the mattress and pulling them out when a wash is due. Thank goodness she hasn't thought of doing a spot-check. So far I've got away with it. And I'm thankful she didn't come up with knickers to match. She got plain white cotton briefs from M&S, never the hint of a thong or even a tanga. But I can live with that.

To be fair, Auntie Sue has many good points. For instance, when she found that I really, really, want to be a writer, she found me a couple of very cool books on writing. And she bought me a whole stack of A4 hardback manuscript books, lined pages inside and covers all in different colours – lime green, purple, shocking pink, silver, scarlet etc – and a box of black gel pens with rubber grips.

"Use them for whatever you like," she said. "Stories, or ideas. Or a journal. I understand that journalling is very important for a writer."

I already kept a journal of sorts in tatty exercise books. I loved these new books, couldn't help gloating over the zingy colours, the feel and smell of the paper, the expanses of pristine lined pages just waiting to be written on. I think I will be an old-fashioned kind of writer, working best with the feeling of connection from brain to hand to pen to paper. Of course it will all go on the computer later. Maybe at the first edit. I've already started using the first book, the shocking pink one. So, thanks Auntie Sue. She also persuaded me to send in one of my short stories to the local county magazine, which is quite a posh glossy one. So I did.

It won't get anywhere, of course, but at least I should get a rejection slip. I've heard that most really famous writers have enough rejection slips to paper whole rooms. Maybe I could start on the downstairs toilet with mine.

So Auntie Sue has her advantages, and I love her really and quite like being with her. But not 24/7. So when Amber rang on Wednesday morning and asked if I fancied a hike in the country, I was definitely up for it. It was too nice a day to be indoors. Peter was off for the week on a football trip, and I thought Auntie Sue might have other ideas, but she was fine with it.

"I'll do you a packed lunch, shall I? And make sure you have enough warm clothes, and stout sensible shoes. A bit of fresh air and exercise will do you the world of good."

Auntie Sue is great really. We are lucky to have her and I really hope she stays a long time. I'm sure we can come to some compromise about underwear and suchlike. I gave her a big hug before I went to rummage in the hall cupboard for my rucksack and hiking boots.

two

I met Amber at her house and we went on together to Willow's, avoiding the town centre as lots of Beechwood

High people might be about and we did look a bit conspicuous in our hiking gear.

"All we need is a coiled-up rope and one of those walking pole things," said Amber. Hamlet was well excited about going walking, panting and grinning a big doggy grin. He's growing fast, changing from a fluffy little thing into quite a long-legged dog, though nobody is quite sure what mixture of breeds he might be.

Willow was waiting at the end of her road, looking elegant even in khaki combats and big boots, hair stuffed up under a green beanie. We headed for the river and the walk alongside it, which is really an overgrown disused railway line shaded by tall trees. Fallen leaves were thick underfoot, the ones still on the trees were gorgeous shades of russet and yellow and brown, and there were shiny conkers under a horse-chestnut tree. Hamlet had a great time snuffling in the leaves and sniffing out scents along the ditches. The air was cool and crisp and made you feel you could walk for hours.

"Better than school, wouldn't you say?" asked Willow, and I agreed, mentally thanking whoever it was had put a match to the place. It was a shame that Rach and Annie weren't here as well.

We followed the river walk until it left the trees behind and led out into open ground, a big river meadow with the footpath running through. Then we took another path that led away from the town and river and into farmland. The path rose gently, and after a while we took a rest and looked down on the houses, a huddle of roofs and streets with the tower of St John's poking up among them.

"And I can see Beech Bank," said Amber, pointing to the long low building at the end of the avenue of beeches.

"And there's Rachel's house, at the end of that windy lane," said Willow.

I didn't think I'd ever walked as far along this path before. Soon we'd left the river meadows and the path was taking us through cultivated farmland, where big machines were working. We stopped in a gateway and watched for a little while. A giant of a machine was harvesting potatoes, digging them out of the ground and sending them skittering in a red-brown cascade into the waiting trailer. So fast did the trailers fill that five or six were in the field at the same time, empty ones coming to take the places of the ones heaped with potatoes being carried away.

I began to imagine the way I would describe the scene in my pink journal that evening; brown furrows left where the harvester had dug, the earthy smell of turned soil and diesel fumes, the feel of autumn sunshine on our faces, taste of dust on our lips, the roar of big machines. I read in one of Auntie Sue's books that a writer uses all her senses to record what she sees.

"Chloe! Chlo–ee!" Amber was waving her hands in front of my face.

"She's composing again, or visualising, or whatever it is writers do," said Willow.

Hamlet was tugging at his lead and whining. They all wanted to move on.

"This must be one of the farms where the migrant kids' families work," said Willow, as we moved away from the gateway to let one of the tractors pass. It roared out of the field and off along a rutted track, with a few potatoes spilling out into the ditch. I picked one up and held it in my hand – smooth and cool, creamy brown with bits of red earth clinging to it.

"Must be," said Amber. "I wonder where the farm itself is. And the camp. The camp must be somewhere near."

A little further on we had our answer. Keeping to the footpath, we walked through a clump of ash and hazel and saw the farm, a huddle of large concrete buildings, with the laden tractor and trailer travelling along a wide farm track towards it. And further yet, across another field and a dip in the hillside, we saw the light-coloured roofs of what looked like a seaside caravan park.

"That must be the camp," said Amber, sounding excited.

"What a pity the footpath doesn't go that way," said Willow. "I'd love to take a look. We might see some of the kids from school. Maybe Madalina."

"We could wander over that way. And say we'd lost track of the footpath, if anyone said anything," suggested Amber, with a sideways glance at Willow. Willow gave her a direct look back. I knew she was going to say that would be a dishonest thing to do, and to remember we're Christians, blah blah. She'd be right, of course. But now and then it surely didn't hurt to bend the rules a bit. I'd like a closer look at that camp myself.

Before she could say anything, the matter was taken out of our hands. Something must have caught Hamlet's eye over in the gateway to the camp, because he suddenly burst into furious yapping and tore off in that direction, with Amber running behind hanging on to the lead.

I must mention that Hamlet is not what he seems. Get him on his own and he's a real cowardy-custard, couldn't say boo to a goose, would run and hide from a mouse. But when he's with Amber, he makes out he's this big bold guard-dog, defending her from all danger and acting aggressive as anything. He thinks nobody has worked out the truth, that it's she who protects *him*, the idiot!

Now, as he ran yapping across the field and towards the gate where the caravans were, we all saw a huge, rough-coated dog appear on the other side of the gate, snarling horribly and baring its teeth and making little runs at the gate. It could have eaten up Hamlet for breakfast, and Hamlet knew it. He stopped dead in his tracks and looked wildly around for Amber, and when he saw that she was there at the end of his lead, doubled back and dived behind her, wrapping the lead round her ankles. Amber stumbled and almost fell, but managed to stay upright and keep hold of the lead. She reassured poor quivering Hamlet, the big wuss, while all the time the other dog raged at them from behind the gate. Then a man appeared from a caravan and spoke softly to the dog, which quietened at once and slunk out of sight. The man stood there, just looking at us.

I wanted to get away from there, fast. But Amber is made of sterner stuff. She likes a bit of drama, does Ams. Holding Hamlet on a tight lead, she walked towards the man.

"Amber, let's go," called Willow, but Amber didn't hear or maybe didn't choose to. Willow and I looked at each other. Nothing for it but to go over there too.

The man was just standing there silently, as though defending his territory. I was a bit scared but my mind was busy working overtime trying to describe him – dark skinned (swarthy), black hair going grey, red neckerchief. Sinister? A bit, maybe, but more defensive and suspicious. Threatening? Not sure, but I felt I wouldn't want to get in an argument with him.

Amber was plunging in head first though. "Good morning, I'm so sorry about my dog. Isn't it a lovely day?"

The man grunted some reply, regarding her watchfully out of narrowed eyes, dark as the sloes on the blackthorn bush near the gate. He wore a check shirt with a waistcoat over baggy cord trousers, worn boots, a shapeless old hat and had a thick blackthorn stick in his hand. The word "gypsy" came into my mind. Behind him, I noticed two or three boys come from behind the other caravans and watch us silently. I thought I recognised a couple of the Year Sevens from school. A line of washing stretched from the blackthorn bush to the nearest caravan and flapped in the breeze.

Willow gave Amber's arm a tug. "Come on, Ams." But Amber wasn't finished yet. "Er – you must be from the farm over there." He didn't answer, and I wondered if perhaps he spoke no English. I also wondered why he was not at work. Then I noticed that the hand holding the stick was covered with a rough bandage, showing some bloodstains. He'd obviously had an accident and was off work.

Amber was blundering on. "I think some of the children here go to our school. There's a girl in our class. Madalina. Do you know her?"

I saw a reaction on the man's face. His sloe-black eyes narrowed even more and his lips tightened. Then he said "No. No Madalina. No one here."

He wanted us to go. We were definitely not welcome here. The man made a slight clicking sound with his mouth and the big dog appeared again, eyeing us and showing his teeth. It was time to go, so we went, led by a very chastened Hamlet who wanted to put as much space as possible between himself and the other dog.

We looked back when we reached the footpath. The man and dog were still standing at the gate watching us silently, and they stood there until we were out of sight behind another clump of trees.

We paused for a moment to recover ourselves. "Well, what do you make of that, then?" asked Amber. "Bit weird, wouldn't you say?"

"Not really," said Willow. "Just a man a bit cheesed off with some nosey girls poking about. Don't blame him, really. And what about not talking to strange men?"

"Well, I was forced into it, more or less," said Amber. "Didn't like his dog though. And I'm a bit disappointed he didn't know Madalina."

"I expect there are other camps," said Willow. "Obviously that's not hers."

Something had been tugging at the back of my mind. "I'm not so sure," I said slowly, and suddenly I knew what the something was. On the washing line, among the work trousers and shirts and towels, there had been a long, droopy blue skirt, the kind Madalina wore to school, with a small burn mark near the hem that I'd noticed on hers.

three

Of course, we were buzzing with speculation for the rest of the day, as we climbed higher towards where the farmland gave way to sheep-grazed common ground, with the slopes of the Bluff towering above. We ate our sandwiches under a hawthorn tree covered with crimson berries, and then walked back to town on the other footpath, the one that passed through more woods than farmland. It had been a lovely day, and the encounter with the sinister man had added extra spice.

"Why would he say that Madalina wasn't there, that he didn't know her?" Amber wondered for the umpteenth time.

We had no answers, but a lot of theories. A little further along the trail, Amber had another idea. "Maybe she's here against her will."

"You mean kidnapped?" said Willow. "Isn't that a bit far-fetched? She does go to school, after all."

"Yes, I know, but that could be cover. She always looks scared half to death, and hardly talks to anyone. She speaks good English though. You do hear about terrible things, like children used as slaves."

We pondered that for a while. We'd been shocked to find that the stuff in some of our favourite High Street shops had been made by young girls paid next to nothing, and that's why the shops could sell it so cheaply. Could something like that be happening on our very doorstep?

"Where was Madalina today then?" asked Amber.

"Working on the farm?" suggested Willow. "There was nobody much at the camp, except a couple of kids too young to work."

We pondered again in silence for a minute or two, our boots swishing through the fallen leaves. "It was definitely her skirt on the line," I said. "She is there somewhere."

"Maybe she's been murdered," said Amber, taking off on a new tack. "That man had a blood-soaked bandage on his hand. Maybe there was a desperate struggle and she put up a fight."

Even I thought that was a bit OTT. The bandage hadn't exactly been blood-soaked, just a few smears. Made me shudder though at the thought. All of a sudden, I wanted to be home, with Auntie Sue stirring something on the cooker and asking if I'd had a good day, and to change my shoes immediately if my feet were wet.

"We can't just leave it like that, though," said Amber. "Can we? Oughtn't we to see if Madalina needs help?"

Willow's phone played its little tune. It was her mum, asking if she would be home before long, and telling her there was no school tomorrow either.

"Tell you what," said Willow. "No school again, so how about we all meet up round at mine tomorrow. Annie and Rachel too. Then we can talk things through and see if there's any way we can think of to help Madalina. We need to pray about it too. OK?"

Willow always tries to keep the rest of us from getting too carried away. If she was on the Jeremy Kyle show he would call her the Voice of Reason. We said OK. It was as good a plan as any, I thought.

We all turned up at Willow's next day, Rachel too. We'd asked Annie as well, but it seemed she wanted to stay in until BB time. I had a feeling Rachel knew something more about Annie that she wasn't telling, but she never breathed a word. Rachel's eyes nearly popped out when we told her what had happened yesterday. For a while we all buzzed with ever more fantastic theories, until Willow reminded us that we ought to be praying. That quietened us down and concentrated our minds a bit. Then we decided on some contingency plans. First Contingency Plan (if Madalina was in school tomorrow), we would:

1. Make an effort to really be friends and get her to trust us.
2. Try to find out about her circumstances without being unduly nosey, inquisitive, pushy or threatening to her (a tall order as there was every likelihood we'd be all of those things, some of us more than others).
3. Try and get her to confide in us (very unlikely if we failed at point 2).

Second Contingency Plan (if Madalina was *not* in school tomorrow.) This created a lot of thought and some heated discussion, as we all had our own ideas. Eventually we decided on:

1. We would make discreet enquiries among the other migrant kids.
2. We would look in the local papers for any news of missing kids or suspicious happenings at the migrant camps, or any bodies discovered recently. Willow vetoed that last bit as being too far-fetched.

There was also 3: make another visit to the migrant camp to see what we could see (Amber's idea) but this was not picked up on, to my great relief, remembering that dog and his fearsome fangs.

From then on, we would have to play it by ear.

As it happened, Contingency Plan Two was not needed, because Madalina was there next day, in a new outfit. Possibly that explained why her blue skirt had been in the wash. Was there really some mystery, or were we letting our fevered imaginations run away with us, as Willow put it?

We got a chance to talk to her at dinner time, and she told us a little about herself. She's actually a Romany gypsy! It didn't seem likely that she'd been kidnapped or used as a slave worker. We wondered if the man had been her uncle. Strange that he'd denied all knowledge of her though. Anyway, there wasn't as much time to talk as we'd have liked. It would all have to go on the back-burner for now, because it was Friday and the mysterious big night at Beech Bank was first and foremost in all our minds.

four

All of us got dressed up to the nines for Beech Bank that evening, pulling out all the stops, because we hadn't a clue who or what was in store, and we reckoned it's as well to be prepared for anything. I wore the green top and cool jeans my brother had bought for my birthday, and Auntie Sue complimented me and never said a word about vests. (Although she did remind me to take a warm coat, as the evenings are getting really cold.) Its dark early now, too.

Lights were blazing at BB, and people were milling about already, even though we'd taken care to go early. Sadie's "reverse psychology" had worked well; just about all the regular kids had turned up, plus several more, just to see what was going on. The big room was already filling up fast, with an excited buzz of conversation filling the air. Microphones set up, but no band or musical instruments in sight. There was a big screen up on stage. A film, then. Intriguing.

If we expected an evening of scintillating entertainment, we soon found we'd been wrong. Different, though. Dead on time, the lights dimmed, the noise hushed and Rod walked onto the stage and took the mike.

"Good evening everyone. Welcome to Beech Bank. This evening, we're showing a short but significant film, but before we do that, I'd like you to meet some of the team who have been involved with the project you'll see, and other projects like it."

First up was a young(ish) man, late twenties, early thirties, nice-looking, dark, who said his name was Clark. He explained about the Aid Mission he worked with and what it did – sought out remote places in poor countries where other agencies normally didn't go, mainly because it would be expensive, too time-consuming or too dangerous to reach them. Like villages deep in the African bush, remote mountain settlements, tribes who lived along jungle rivers or even in war zones. Often these places could only be reached by helicopter, or canoe, or overland in tough 4x4s. There was danger and difficulty, it was hard and exhausting and often discouraging work, but they were reaching people who had never been reached before, not only with supplies and medical aid, but with the message that God loved them and that Jesus had died for their salvation.

You could hear a pin drop. Clark introduced the rest of the team – four of them, all younger guys in their gap year, using the time not to backpack round the world but to get involved with this stuff which was even more exciting. They each spoke a few words – Ed, Matt, Stuart and Jay – and explained why they had chosen to do this. All of them were fit guys, and, by his accent, Jay was American. I noticed Willow in particular couldn't keep her eyes off him and I didn't blame her – startling blue eyes in a tanned face, thick blonde hair, shoulders that looked like he was a sportsman. Casual sporty gear. I bet Willow was glad she'd worn her newest top and skinny jeans. In fact, I knew we were all patting ourselves on the back for making the effort.

My mind was wandering a bit, so I forced myself to concentrate. When the film started, though, nobody had a problem with concentration. We were all mesmerised.

It kicked off with shots of a jeep ploughing its way through tall grass on rough ground, plunging and bucking over deep ruts and high ridges, almost stalling and then getting going again, pressing into wild terrain where no vehicle had gone before. A narrator on board explained that they were searching for a certain tiny village hidden in the African bush.

And then they found it, bursting suddenly into a kind of clearing, with a few rough huts. Almost deserted. I don't know where the people were, maybe they'd hidden themselves out of camera range. Except for two children, a boy and a girl. They couldn't run and they couldn't hide. They were lying out on the bare sandy ground in baking sunshine, wearing only tattered shirts, lying on their stomachs and raising their heads to look at the cameras with huge, sad, bewildered eyes in beautiful little faces. The narrator told us they were actually five and seven, but they were no bigger than toddlers. They were badly malnourished, and their skinny, stick-like little legs gave evidence that they were polio victims, unable to walk.

I found I was holding my breath, twisting the hem of my top round and round in my hands. Annie next to me reached out and grabbed my hand, and we locked our fingers together, silently willing someone to come and help the children. Why had they been left lying there all alone on the bare ground?

Then suddenly, the little boy turned his head and a gleam of hope came into his eyes. The cameras panned across the clearing, where we saw the tall grasses part, and another small girl walk out. The narrator said this little girl was the elder sister of the two on the ground, eight years old, but tiny for her age. She wore a big baggy shirt to her ankles and was lugging a yellow plastic drum almost as big as herself. The narrator explained that it held water from a source some distance away. He said that all the children were severely malnourished and there was little food to be had, but the elder sister had walked miles to get the only thing she could for her brother and sister, water.

I had a huge lump in my throat, which seemed to get bigger and bigger as I watched. She didn't even take a rest. First, she helped each of them to drink. Then, she set about bathing them, grubby as they were from lying half-naked on the bare earth. Each in turn, the little girl picked up and carried her siblings to a patch of grass, where she carefully poured water over one emaciated little body. Someone, maybe the camera crew, produced liquid soap, which she lathered and used to wash the child clean, ignoring their feeble protests. Then rinsed. Then carried the child to a blanket laid out on the ground, again provided by the crew. Covered the child with a towel. Repeated the process with the other child, her little face set and determined. The camera crew produced cookies. The little girl first gave a cookie to each of her siblings, only then taking one for herself, though she must have been desperately hungry too.

By now the tears were running down my face, and there were gulps and sniffs all over the room. The narrator explained that the little eight year old was the sole carer and provider for her family.

The film ended and the lights came on. All of us had been drawn into the scene; we just had to know what happened to that family. Rod asked the same question, after thanking Clark for his presentation.

"They were helped," said Clark quietly. "The two little ones with health problems were taken to a hospital where they received the medical help they needed, then went to a foster family in another village, where there's a clinic, so they will continue to get the help they need.

They're doing well. The older sister moved in with them too. She's going to school and learning to be a child again."

He paused, and then went on, "We present this film as an example of the work we're doing, of the people we're trying to help. Powerful stuff, wouldn't you say? The way that little girl worked and sacrificed for her family speaks volumes, doesn't it? Now, does anyone else have questions?"

five

Well, there were plenty. Once the kids got started, the questions came thick and fast. How old did you have to be to get on one of those teams? Could anyone go? Did you have to be specially trained? How was it all paid for?

He answered each one patiently and thoroughly. Yes, they were always, always, in need of more people to work on the teams. It varied, but usually you had to be eighteen at least. A lot of young people used their gap year to help, like these four guys here. Yes, girls went too. No, you had a time of basic training but you didn't have to be necessarily qualified in anything. Qualified people were always desperately needed though – nurses, doctors, pharmacists, teachers, technicians, agricultural workers – just about everyone with a skill that could be used and shared. You had to provide your own money for the trip, fundraising for yourself if need be. You had to be fit and healthy. A driver's licence was an advantage. You had to be prepared to work long hard hours and not be afraid of getting your hands dirty.

It sounded very tough. But, seeing the actual kids on the film, realising they were people with personalities and problems and needs that we could maybe make a difference to, had made it all so real. I'd had tough times in my own life and thought I knew a bit about suffering. But now I knew I was one of the fortunate ones. And I desperately wanted to rise to the challenge this evening had brought.

There was food and coffee afterwards, and the five team members mingled with us kids, chatting about anything else we wanted to know. All of us had been affected by this evening.

"I really, really, want to get on one of those teams," said Amber, balancing a plate of sausage rolls and crisps.

"Not much chance, for a few years at least," I said ruefully.

"At least four years, till we get to our gap years," said Rachel.

"We could raise funds though, couldn't we?" said Annie. "I mean, we've got to do *something*."

Fundraising sounded rather a dull prospect, when what we wanted was to be out there, travelling and working, making a difference.

"It'll probably take us four years to save for what we'd

need anyway," said Amber, rather pessimistically for her.

"Where's Willow?" asked Rachel, looking round suddenly.

We soon saw her, across the crowded room, her auburn hair standing out under the lights like a flame. She was deep in conversation with the blonde American boy, whose fair hair gleamed like silk. They made a striking couple.

"Ooh la la!" said Rachel wryly. "Willow didn't waste much time! I thought she was against casual flirtations."

"Maybe it's not a casual flirtation," said Amber. "Maybe their eyes met across a crowded room, and all was lost."

We giggled.

"He's a fit guy, though, you have to admit," Amber went on. "Knows how to dress too. Not like some." She waved a hand dismissively towards the group of local lads, mostly bunched together in their usual uniforms of hoodies and track bottoms or low-slung jeans. "Although I must say I didn't think Wills was that shallow that she'd be impressed by chinos with creases in them and Converse trainers." They giggled again.

"You're a bit quiet, Chloe," said Annie suddenly.

I had been listening to the conversation with only half an ear. I just couldn't get my mind off those poor kids on the screen. It had really fired me up, and I just didn't see how I could possibly wait four whole years to do something about it. I tried to explain this to the others and they became serious again, but it was getting late and people were beginning to leave.

We walked home together part of the way, the five of us, our minds still buzzing with the evening. Willow's eyes held a sparkle under the street lights, and when Amber mentioned Jay, her cheeks got faintly pink.

"Did you swap numbers?" asked Amber innocently.

"Not exactly," said Willow. "Actually, Clark and Jay, and that dark-haired one, Matt, are staying over at the Vicarage for a couple of nights, so they'll be in church Sunday morning."

"Cool," said Rachel. "You two seemed to be hitting it off, Wills. Might be a little something going on, not?"

"Not," said Willow. "We were talking over the project, actually, that's all. And school. He's doing English Lit for his major."

"His which?"

"His major. They have a main subject they major in at uni – only they call it college – and then another one a bit less important, the minor. He might go into relief aid work full time after commencement. That's graduation, for the benefit of you guys who may not know. He comes from Riveroak in Tennessee. His father runs a hardware store. That's a place where they sell tools and paint and DIY stuff . . ."

"Yes, yes, we know what a hardware store is," said Amber. "I must say you found out an awful lot in just a few minutes. Any more info? Brothers? Sisters? Dogs? Sports teams? Favourite food? Burgers, I bet, that's what Americans mostly eat, isn't it?"

"Oh, shut up," said Willow. "You're only jealous!"

And there might have been a bit of truth in that. I thought that Willow was speaking with a bit of an American twang too, but I decided it might be verging on bitchy to point it out.

Anyway, an idea had suddenly occurred to me as I walked along. My mind was in overdrive, and I had a thought that came like a flash of light. It would be years before we could go to Africa or any of the developing countries on projects, but maybe there was something we could do here and now. We had a migrant population right here on our doorstep, a mission field in itself. And we already had a contact in Madalina. "Do what you can, and don't worry about what you can't" was something that Rod sometimes told us. And we could do something. I'd just thought what. Not something big – something *major* – but maybe something that would be a start.

"School uniform!" I said.

They all stopped and looked at me. Willow said, "They don't normally wear school uniform in the States." However much she protested, her mind was definitely on Jay!

"No, I mean for Madalina," I said. "We don't have to wait for four years to make a difference to someone, *we can do it right now!* You know how Madalina wears those awful old granny clothes, and then that stuff today that was really cheap and nasty, right?" One or two of them nodded. "Well, if she had uniform, it might do a lot for her confidence. Help her not to stand out so much. She wouldn't be so scared of being picked on."

They were getting the point now. Annie said, "And we could get school uniform for her, couldn't we? We know her size. We've all had new stuff the beginning of the year. I haven't worn half mine yet. We could all contribute something. We'd never miss it. Good thinking, Clo."

The others were catching on, remembering stuff they'd got in drawers still in their wrappings. I thought of all the new tights and underwear in my own drawers. Between us we could get Madalina all kitted out in nice new stuff, and never even miss any of it.

"Let's do it," said Rachel. "We can get together tomorrow."

There was a chorus of approval. We'd reached the junction where Amber and I branched off from the others, and we parted on a big high.

Auntie Sue gave the impression that she was waiting up for me, though it was barely 10 yet. I pointed out that there's only a block or two between Amber's house and ours, but she said that girls have been known to disappear just yards from their own front door.

"You look as though you've enjoyed yourself," she said, and I said, "We had a great night. The best ever," and went to see what was in the fridge. It *had* been a good night at Beech Bank, challenging, exciting, inspiring. And we had something to work on.

Two more good things happened before the weekend was out.

1. Auntie Sue decided she would stay on with us, as we have plenty of room and the present economic climate isn't conducive to house buying. So she's with us, indefinitely. Yay! And I really mean that.

2. I heard back from the glossy mag my story went to. Not an acceptance, but not quite a rejection either. A nice letter saying my story wasn't quite what they wanted, but that it showed great promise, and maybe I'd like to try again after studying the enclosed guidelines. So I reckon that, even if my feet are not exactly on the bottom rung of the writing career ladder yet, they soon will be! Yay again!

PART FOUR

Madalina's Story

LIVING THE DREAM

one

What is a friend? A *mora*, as we would say in our Romany tongue? I never knew what it really meant before I came here. Where I lived, there were family, there were others like us, and there were people not like us. The *gadja*. Anyone not gypsy.

Mostly, it was family. All of us lived close together, separate from the rest of the village where we had settled, in houses built around a central courtyard. When I say houses, they were not like the houses here, which seem much more like the beautiful homes you see on foreign TV programmes. Our houses were small boxes, mostly of concrete blocks, two or three rooms linked together by doorways, sometimes with doors but often curtains. When someone married or children were born, another room would be added on, provided enough money could be obtained to buy the concrete blocks and other building materials. We had electricity, though at times the power failed. There was TV and an electric waffle-maker, my mother's pride and joy. The TV was mostly switched on, though no one paid much attention to the programmes. Except me.

All of us lived here: my father and mother, my four younger brothers and sisters, my uncle, his wife and their three boys, my grandfather and my grandmother. My grandfather was an old man now, but he still believed that he was the head of the family, that everyone must listen to what he had to say.

"The sun is shining," he would say, one bright morning in springtime. "The foreigners will be coming. Time to take the goods down to the market and make sales."

The "goods" were a wide variety of things, some articles fashioned of wood and metal, other items collected, bartered for and gathered by various family members and then hopefully sold to foreign tourists as memorabilia. People were sometimes willing to pay good money for something beautiful we had made and painted, sometimes they paid enormous prices for rubbish. When this happened, my grandfather would rub his hands with glee, count out the money, put most of it away but give some to my mother and aunt and tell them to buy best mutton for a good stew. They mostly bought what they thought was the best value. Grandmother would examine the meat when it came, poke and prod it, discuss and criticise and finally cook it.

It was Grandmother who was the real head of the household. Elderly gypsy women have great status and are respected by all and feared by some. Most in our household feared Grandmother, not least her sons and daughters-in-law. My aunt and my mother were the ones who did all the work, all the cooking, cleaning, washing and caring for six adults and seven children, mostly in the courtyard and under the eagle eye of my grandmother. The men were out and about on their own business, buying and selling, dealing and bartering. When they were home they whittled pieces of wood, fashioning pine and ash into spoons and ladles, clothes pegs, wooden plates, decorative eggs, pipes, tiny mugs and cups. These were often painted in bright colours and wonderful decorative patterns.

"We are craftsmen and artisans," my father or my uncle would declare proudly. "We are not labourers." And it's true, they make beautiful things.

So it was the women who laboured, from first light until darkness fell, cooking on the stove in the yard, heating water for the washing of pots and pans, of clothes and bedding, and occasionally the children too. The women who fetched water from the well, who shopped in the market, who sold the articles made by the men.

The children went to school, sometimes. Often, they didn't. As soon as the boys were old enough, they joined in the activities of the men. Gypsies were not welcome in school, and they did not like going.

"These gypsy brats are not quite human," I overheard one teacher say to another on my very first day there. "Scarcely above animal level, most of them. Their intelligence is low. Their speech is different, they cannot pick up and follow the lessons. Most don't last long."

And most didn't. They gave up and stayed home. The *gadja* children resented us. They avoided us, as their elders avoided our families. We were dirty, we were vermin, they said. Quite often there was violence. We had heard that whole gypsy encampments had been burned out in other places, in order to "cleanse" the area.

So school was not a pleasant place to be if you were a gypsy. Yet school was the one thing that I yearned for, longed for, struggled to attend.

It all began when my uncle came home one day with a handcart of goods he had picked up from some contact he had run into. The assorted items were picked over and sorted in order of their usefulness, or, preferably, saleability. There were shoes, which everyone tried on in turn, pushing their feet in regardless of fit or style. We children often went barefoot, and any shoes, however ill-fitting or unsuitable, were better than none. My small sister, Katya, had a pair of too-small pink satin ballet slippers and my nine-year-old brother a pair of trainers several sizes too large. Both were delighted.

Anything saleable was put on one side for the market. My Aunt Isabel seized on a pair of blue and white china jugs and declared she must keep them for her shelves, despite the chip in one of them. My mother claimed an intricate silver photo frame, though we had no photos to go into it. "Maybe one day," she said optimistically and placed it on top of the TV set.

There were a few toys, divided among the children. And a book, which I seized on and pulled from the cart. Lines of words, indecipherable to me but all saying something, telling some tale. I longed to know what the words said.

"What is that book?" demanded my grandmother, holding out a bony hand as brown and gnarled as a walnut. I knew and feared that hand. Had felt it many times connect with my bare legs in a slap, or the bony fingers pinch my cheeks or my upper arms. I handed it to her. She examined it, flicked the pages, turned it around to look at the spine and covers, gave a small disdainful spit into the dusty ground. "Poof! Not worth much! It's foreign. Try it in the market, if it doesn't sell, it'll light the fire."

I gave a cry and sprang forward, snatching the book from her. "Oh, please, let me keep it! Please!"

She gave me a keen look from beady black eyes. "We do not need a book. We have a book already." She gestured towards a shelf, where a tattered copy of *Anna Karenina* sat between a lustre vase and a pottery model of a carthorse.

"But I need it!" I said desperately. I was surprised at my own daring: nobody argued with my grandmother. She was surprised too, even speechless for a moment. My Uncle Stefan, curious at my outburst, came and took the book from me. Uncle Stefan is a clever man, quick not only at numbers, as are most gypsies, but also quick to pick up other tongues. He understands some Hungarian, Romanian and English as well as our own Roma language, and can even speak a little of these tongues. He said "This is an English book. It is by William Shakespeare. *A Winter's Tale*. Why do you want it?"

I didn't quite know myself and couldn't explain. I just felt that somehow, some day, I might learn what those words on the page said. I tried to tell them this, which caused my grandmother to snort. But she did not object when my uncle said, "Let her keep the book then."

I took the book and hid it in my sleeping place, under my blanket. Sometimes I took it out and smoothed the covers with my fingers, turning the pages and pretending I could read the words. They made no sense to me, line after line of black letters on the page. But one day I would read them. Somehow, I would learn, I would listen, I would understand, I would make sense of it all, I would read. I would do it.

two

I was turning out to be a great disappointment to my family. My grandmother disapproved strongly of my desire for school, my bookishness, and the fact that I would sit in front of the TV set watching a whole programme from start to finish. I learned so much from those programmes, about other parts of the world, other ways of living, other kinds of people, and I was fascinated by it all. My grandmother could not understand my interest.

"We have all we need to know, passed on from father to son, and mother to daughter. We have our own music, our own stories and dances, our own craftsmanship."

"Yes and I love all that, but our way is not the only

way. There is so much more in the world, so much to learn and find out."

"And none of it much good! The rest of the world is not for us. They don't want us anyway. We are of no value to them. We must make our own way, use our wits and keep one step ahead. We keep ourselves to ourselves. It is our way."

My grandmother was a stubborn woman, and I had inherited her stubbornness. I went to school whenever I could, and fretted in the winter months when I could not go because snow was thick on the ground and I had no proper stout boots or warm clothing. I watched television as long as the power held out. My family was proud of its TV set and kept it on at all hours to impress the neighbours. I read whenever and whatever I could, school books, newspapers I picked up discarded in the street, government pamphlets, cheap magazines. And slowly but surely, I was picking up a little English from Uncle Stefan.

But one of the most vexed questions in the family was that of my marriage. Most Roma girls marry young, 13 or 14, their parents choosing and promising them to sons from another Roma family, often from childhood. I had stubbornly refused to consider marriage. I wanted to marry one day, have my own family. But not yet. Not until I had learned to read English and other languages, and seen what else was in the world. And I would choose my own husband.

My grandmother shook her head and blamed my mother for not punishing me enough when I was younger. "She has a rebellious spirit. It should have been broken long before this. Now she will be trouble."

Trouble or not, I was not about to be tied down for life yet, as my mother and aunt were, or dragged down by a gaggle of children before I was 20.

My family had mixed feelings, even my grandmother. They would have loved a wedding celebration, with the music, the dancing, the feasting, the presents and days of merrymaking. But there was the little matter of my *cheiz* – my dowry – which would have to be managed somehow, and times were hard. The matter was left for the time being, simmering beneath the surface.

So it was like a shaft of light when my Uncle Stefan came in one day with shining eyes and excitement lightening his step. He had met someone who was looking for workers to go to the UK. There were opportunities now for more and more Eastern Europeans to go there for the harvest season, first picking soft fruit, then apples and pears, then potatoes. They didn't mind about the workers being gypsies, the money was excellent, camps were provided for the families, with every comfort. They would return at the end of the season with much money in their pockets. Uncle Stefan intended to take his whole family and make his fortune.

His announcement caused pandemonium. My cousins were wildly excited, Aunt Isabel thrown into confusion, torn between leaving the familiar with its security of a kind, and curiosity about this new venture which would provide escape for a time and a chance

for a change from the dull and hard routine. My
mother looked forlorn. She would lose her sister-
in-law, co-worker and confidante. My grandparents
did not approve. "You may not come back," said my
grandfather darkly.

"Yes, yes, we will come back when the work finishes,"
my uncle assured him. "That is the agreement. And
with all of us working, much the richer!"

In the end, it was the prospect of the money that
sweetened the pill. Most of the families I know love
money, gather it, boast of it, flaunt it and often quickly
spend it. The thought of Uncle Stefan and his family
returning with a fortune was enough to make even my
grandmother hold her tongue.

My father said, "Well, good luck to you, and I wish
I'd been the one to meet that man. As it is . . ." he broke
off with a regretful shrug of the shoulders. It went
without saying that one of the sons had to stay with the
old folks. "If only one of my boys were older, he could
have gone with you," he added ruefully.

It was then that the idea sprang into my mind like a
beam of sunlight. "I could go with you! I'm old enough
to work!"

Everybody looked at me, some with mouths dropped
open. Nobody spoke for a moment, and in that moment
my head was whirling with possibilities. I could work,
certainly I could. But I could also go to school! A good
school, an English school, where there was freedom and
equality and tolerance of all. I held my breath. Then
they all began to speak.

"You! You are a girl! They will not take girls!"

"It would not be safe! You would be in danger! You would mix with *gadja*!"

"Nobody would want to marry you, even if you did come back!"

I let out my breath and said in a rush, "I would be safe! I would be with Uncle Stefan and Aunt Isabel! I would work hard when I was not in school . . ."

"School?"

"I might have known! With her, always books, always school! There is something badly wrong with that girl!"

"She means never to come back! I knew it!"

They were off again. But I looked across at my uncle, and he closed one eye in a wink. My heart leapt! He would take me, if I could only get the others to agree. Oh, they must!

There was a lot more loud discussion, with much raising of voices and some tears. My grandmother finally said, "Well then, if there is to be no peace, we must let her go. But it is a sad thing, when a girl, the comfort of her grandparents in their old age, wishes to desert her family."

She wiped her eyes with the fringes of her shawl. Comfort indeed! She'd shown very little affection to me over the years, the old witch, and I had mainly avoided her whenever possible, which wasn't often, considering the way we lived.

"I will ask the Gangmaster tomorrow," said my uncle. "It isn't certain he will agree, but I will ask."

Suddenly, across the small room, I caught my mother's eye. She hadn't spoken a word in all the commotion. She looked stricken, and my own heart gave a great wrench at the thought of leaving her. If she begged me to stay, then I must.

Later in the day, my mother picked up the water buckets and motioned to me to go with her to the well where we draw our water. My mother is always a quiet woman, but now she was even quieter than usual. I felt torn. If my mother needed me to stay, I would. It would be a hard time for her, with half the household gone and all the work upon her shoulders.

We had reached the well. A lilac tree grew beside it, and the pale purple cones of flowers gave off a sweet fragrance. My mother put down the buckets and turned to face me, gripping me by both shoulders. She looked deep into my eyes, with brown eyes that already had lines forming around them, though she was barely 30.

"Madalina, if this Gangmaster says yes, and Stefan and Isabel are willing to take you with them, and you want to go, then you must go."

I gasped. I had not expected this. "Mama, do you mean it?"

She nodded and gave me a little shake. "I mean it. You must take the chance. Maybe – maybe it will lead to something – a better life for you."

I felt a lump rise in my throat. "It's only for a while, Mama, I'll come back after harvest, I promise."

She nodded again, looking deeply at me. "I want

more for you, Madalina. You are clever, you will learn. I trust you. You are my good girl."

She had never praised me like this before. We were not much given to hugging, but suddenly we were hugging each other hard, there by the sweet-smelling lilac tree, and the tears were pouring down my cheeks. She had given me the gift of choice. I could only whisper, "Thank you, Mama. Thank you."

After a while she dried both our faces with her apron and picked up the buckets. Life must go on, and tomorrow, as always, there would be meals to cook and washing to be done.

three

I remember very little about the journey here, except that I and my three cousins were all very sick on the boat. I remember being very glad to see the white cliffs of England and to feel firm land under my feet again.

England was not quite as I'd imagined. Some of the countryside was beautiful and very green, but the towns were busy and bewildering, filled with brick and stone houses and glittering shop windows. So many people. The roads were frightening, though fascinating to my cousins. So many vehicles on smooth hard roads, travelling at such speeds! I could not understand how they failed to collide.

"There are many rules," said the Gangmaster knowledgeably. "Many laws, and hard penalties for those who do not keep them."

The Gangmaster travelled with us, a short, stocky man, who, like many short people, liked to be boss. His job suited him well. He knew everything, or pretended to, and looked down on us as being ignorant and none too bright. He was not a cruel man, but took his position very seriously, and woe betide anyone who stepped out of line. He told us, loudly and often, that he would stand no nonsense from the likes of us. He had been reluctant to let me join the workers, arguing that a young girl was a great responsibility and likely to be trouble, but agreeing when Aunt Isabel pleaded to be allowed my help and company in a family of boys and men. I think some money from my uncle may also have helped him to agree.

We were tired, sweaty and dirty when we reached our destination. Many others were there, milling around before being assigned to their camps, all nationalities from Eastern Europe, though not many Roma. Some of them drew apart from us a little, muttering "Gypsies!"

"Why do they do that?" I asked my aunt. "We are no dirtier, or uglier, or more unpleasant smelling than any of them."

Weariness and travel was making me crabby. We'd been pushed to the back while queuing for a drink, and I resented it.

My aunt hushed me. "It's always been so. Accept it, or we might get worse treatment. It's the same everywhere."

Other things weren't quite as I'd expected either. For one thing, I couldn't go to school yet. All British children had school holidays and school would not open again until September. My uncle was rather pleased. We'd all be able to work on the picking of strawberries, raspberries and blackcurrants, instead of wasting time. I'd never known my uncle so keen to get to work.

The camps were rather disappointing too. I'd half-imagined Romany wagons of the kind our folks used to live in, with horses and plenty of space. Instead, we had modern caravans, large enough, considering how crowded we were at home, but parked in a big field with many others. There were "facilities" – toilets, showers, a shop and a leisure place to play games. But another shock came when we found that the money for these conveniences would be taken from our wages.

But it couldn't be helped. So we picked and picked, raspberries, strawberries, blackcurrants, redcurrants, day after day, until our hands were stained with berry juice and our backs ached. Uncle added up the wages, either gloating or complaining, but I longed for the day when I could go to school.

I had to wait and wait. I mentioned it as often as I dared, once the new term had started, but excuses were made and then we picked apples and pears every day until even October was nearly over. Then we moved to a new farm for potato harvest.

I liked the new camp better, there were trees and hills towering over the farmlands in the valley. Our caravan was big, I even had my own little cubicle to sleep in at one end, just room for a narrow bunk with cupboards below and shelves above, but all my own. I carefully hoarded my precious books and read them whenever I had a chance. Uncle grumbled when I reminded him once again that we must be enrolled at school. He would have liked all of us to keep working and earning. But I was determined, and along with others from the camp, we got places at Beechwood High. The younger kids went to the primary school. Strictly speaking, all my cousins should have enrolled too; Luc was 14 and Mihai 15. But nobody asked questions, and the Gangmaster winked his eye at such matters. Neither wanted to go to school anyway. So only 11-year-old Bogdan and I were enrolled at the High School. We started after the half-term holiday.

My aunt fussed, and did not know what we should wear, or take with us. On the first day, she gave us packages of bread and bacon for our lunch. I soon realised that none of the other kids took food, and put mine into a bin. The first day was very difficult. All of us migrants were gathered together and given a little talk by the Head.

"Welcome to Beechwood High," he said in slow and careful English. "We want you to be happy here, but you need to know the rules." And then he told them, a long list that I couldn't quite follow and soon forgot. I wanted to stay with Bogdan or with some of the others from the camp, but I was placed in a class all by myself. A girl was there that I had seen on the school bus, she

smiled at me when Mr Bryce introduced me to the class.
I didn't smile back. I was learning that it was best to
keep quiet and keep my head well down. Because we
soon found that people here were not as friendly as we'd
expected.

It wasn't only the stares, the remarks and the giggles.
We soon found that many of the pupils, boys and girls,
resented us. Some of them were very big, bigger than
Luc and Mihai. They could be very scary when they
made jokes in deep voices and called names. I saw real
hatred in the eyes of some of them, and stayed as far
away from them as possible.

But being in a real British school was worth it all. I
seized eagerly all that was offered me. On the second
day, I had something that I understood was a test of
intelligence. Afterwards, the teacher called another
teacher and they looked together at the results. Then
they both looked at me.

"An excellent result, young lady," said one. "Well
done! Work hard and you'll do well."

As I left the room, I heard him say to the other
teacher, "I think this must be the highest score we've
ever seen here. Remarkable!"

And then there was the fire in school, which made me
so frightened that I hardly knew what to do. The school
was closed for two days. The migrant kids were being
blamed for starting the fire, and I was terrified. Because
they were right. I knew who had started it. I knew it was
Bogdan.

Bogdan has this thing about fire. My grandparents

say it's because he feels in his blood the times when we lived in wagons and moved about, when our lives centred around the campfire. If he gets matches, he might take it into his head to set fire to whatever looks interesting. Once he set the fringes of my grandmother's shawl alight, hanging to dry in the courtyard. Another time he put a match to a trail of paraffin on the ground and nearly caused an explosion in our cooking stove.

"Why do you do it?" asked Uncle Stefan, when Bogdan had singed his eyebrows for the third time.

"I like to," said Bogdan, wrinkling his face with concentration as he tried to explain. "I like the way some things take longer than others to catch light. I like the different colour flames. I like the way the smoke goes up in curls. I want to know how fire works."

"There are places they send children like you," said my uncle ominously. "Shut-in places. You would not like it."

Bogdan did not like the sound of that. He hadn't set a fire lately. Until now.

"I know it was you," I told him that afternoon as we walked across to the camp from where the school bus dropped us. "You had matches this morning. You are so stupid. If they find out . . ." I didn't finish, not wanting to think what might happen – us being beaten up, or barred from school. Or even Uncle Stefan losing his job and being sent home.

Bogdan looked scared too, as though he suddenly realised the seriousness of what he'd done. "Don't tell, will you? I just wanted to see what those shoes would

burn like. They made good black smoke, didn't they?
You could smell the rubber! And they can get more
shoes. They're all rich here."

He was brightening up, beginning to feel quite
pleased with himself again. I gave him a hard shove.
"Stupid! What if they find out and tell your father?"

That took the smile off his face. "You won't tell, will
you?"

"Only if you promise to never, never do that again. I
do not want to be sent away from school."

"School, school, stupid school – that's all you ever
think about! I hate it. I wish I'd burnt it right down to
the ground! I will next time!"

"You will not!" I gave him another shove. I was
bigger than him, and he gave a squawk and promised,
and even handed me his matches. I gave him a chocolate
bar from the camp vending machine, to make up for the
shoves. I was very fond of Bogdan really.

four

Since there was no school, I worked on the farm the next
day with my aunt and cousins, grading the potatoes as
they were tipped on to fast-moving conveyer belts and
picking out the misshapen ones, the damaged ones, the
small stones and bits of debris that came in from the
fields with them. It was tedious, tiring work. The day

before, Uncle Stefan had nicked his hand on a sharp piece of metal and had a deep cut. He had been told to stay off until it was healing. There were strict safety rules, but he was not sorry to miss work for a day or two. My uncle found the work very tedious and would much prefer to be at the camp whittling his wooden artefacts. And I was there to take his place.

That was the day that some of the girls from school visited the camp and asked for me. My uncle was angry about that when we finished work that evening.

"I told them there was nobody of that name here, and I made Rac show his teeth. Why did you invite them here, girl?"

"I didn't invite them," I said wearily. All I wanted was to lie down on my bunk and read for a while. But there was food to prepare, water to boil, later on washing to be done. I went to fill the kettles for my aunt while she began to prepare vegetables. I understood my uncle's secrecy and why he had lied about me. We were aliens in a strange country, and people suspected us gypsies of all kinds of things, sometimes with good reason. The dog, Rac, for instance. My uncle had bought him from a man at another farm, and quickly trained him in the ways he wanted. My uncle had a way with dogs, horses too, a way of whispering into their ears in a certain manner, of bending them to his will. But dogs like Rac aren't allowed here. The secrecy was more than that, though, a suspicion and distrust bred into the Roma through generations of being treated as criminals and outcasts.

My uncle gave me a hard look. "I begin to think

maybe your grandparents were right. Already you are a cause of trouble. Maybe we should not have brought you and let you go to that school."

My aunt gave me the slightest nudge, standing beside me at the little stove. I said, "Sorry, Uncle. It won't happen again."

And I *was* sorry, but only because I thought the girls might not want to be friends with me again. And I was beginning to like those girls.

I needn't have worried though. The day we went back to school they asked me to sit with them at dinner time. They were still friendly and I told them a little about myself. Rachel sat beside me on the bus that afternoon and we chatted until she got off at her stop.

On Saturday it rained, just a short sharp shower, but enough to make the potatoes too wet to be lifted and to go into storage. My uncle carved, my cousins hung around the leisure place, getting up to no good, their parents feared. My aunt announced her intention of going to the town to the Saturday market, and asked me to go along. I jumped at the chance, and when we had done the morning work and had an early dinner, we set off along the footpath, with fallen leaves still damp underfoot.

I was getting very attached to Aunt Isabel. Earlier in the week, she had somehow got hold of new clothes for me: jeans, top and shoes, noticing how I stood out among the other girls here. I'd worn them to school yesterday, grateful for her kindness. Uncle was back at work then, all of them off early before we left for school. Aunt had cautioned me, "Your uncle will not be happy to see you dressed like this, so make sure you're changed before he comes home." I understood. I wanted no more trouble. Bogdan was the only one who would see what I wore to school, and I had enough on him to blackmail him into silence.

I soon realised that the clothes were not quite right – the jeans stiff and too big and not the style the others wore, the top like a boy's, the shoes uncomfortable. I felt only marginally better than before, but I was grateful to my aunt and wouldn't mention a word. But I didn't like the snickers of some of the other girls.

Now I was back in my old clothes, and hoped I wouldn't meet anyone from Beechwood High in town. We'd barely got to the market though when I heard a girl's voice say, "Oh, there's Madalina! Hi, Madalina!"

It was Willow, the flame-haired girl, with Rachel and Annie, browsing round the market stalls. I couldn't avoid them. I introduced my aunt, who ducked her head shyly and smiled. She speaks very little English.

We chatted for a while, standing beside the fresh fish van. My aunt was considering the different kinds of fish, all ice-fresh and gleaming. I will never get used to the variety, the vast choice of food there is here.

Willow suddenly looked at the other two and then at me. "Madalina, would your aunt let you come to my house for a bit? I only live a couple of streets away."

I felt my mouth drop open. Nobody had ever, ever, invited me to their house before, apart from the other Romas back home. "Just for an hour or so," said

Willow, fingering the little phone that all kids carry here. "Amber and Chloe will come round too, if I call them. We've something we'd like to show you."

I looked at her. I should be suspicious, all my instincts told me I should suspect some other motive, but I had a strong feeling that I could trust her. I spoke quickly to my aunt. She looked very doubtful, almost frightened, but then said, "Only one hour, then. I will be here, and will sit over there on that bench when I have finished buying. Not a word to your uncle, you understand. Not one word."

I promised. My heart thumped as I went with the three girls through the streets and into a quieter one, Willow talking on the phone as she went. Her house was at the end. It was bigger than any I'd been in before, and her mother was there, looking rather startled when she saw me, but saying warmly, "Hello, Madalina. It is so nice to meet you."

But Willow's room just took my breath away. It was like something from the movies I saw on TV, a movie star's bedroom. I hardly dared go in.

The others smiled. "Come on in, it's OK. Just Willow's designer style. Come and sit down."

I perched on the edge of a wicker chair. In a moment, Amber and Chloe came bursting in, their hands full of bulging carrier bags. They tipped them onto the bed, and clothes came spilling out.

"We'll get some coffee in a mo," said Willow. "In the meantime, Madalina, we thought you might like to have school uniform the same as ours."

They pulled out other garments from cupboards, on hangers or in plastic bags, new and bright, white shirts, sweaters with the school logo, underwear, a pair of black shoes such as they wore, trousers, a couple of skirts that were so indecently short I knew I'd never dare wear them. All the girls were happy and smiling. I could only splutter, helplessly, "I . . . I do not understand."

"They're for you," said Amber. "Things we don't really need. School things. So you'll be in uniform like us."

I did not know what to think. My head was whirling. I would no longer have to wear the gypsy-ish clothes that called attention and ridicule to myself. I would fit in, be free to study. All of them were beaming at me. I stammered, "But . . . but, I can never pay for all this."

"You don't have to pay," said Willow. "They're a gift. From all of us, to you."

A gift. I was not sure I understood gifts. There was always a price to pay, somewhere, a favour to be called in.

"But . . . what do you want from me?" I asked, bewildered.

"Nothing," said Willow and Rachel together. "Nothing at all." And then Chloe came and gave me a hug, and I was reminded of my mother far away, and suddenly I had tears on my cheeks again.

My aunt was astonished when I joined her carrying bags bulging with school clothes. I explained quickly, and she was as speechless as I had been. Back home we'd sometimes had clothing from aid agencies, but I opened the bags and showed her that these were all brand new.

"I do not understand it," she said.

I didn't really, either, but suddenly I felt glad and light-hearted. I couldn't wait to go to school next week in my new uniform. I was sure I'd learn all the better for it.

We walked home with our bags, plotting how we'd smuggle the new stuff in and hide it away without my uncle noticing. Before long we were giggling as though we were both schoolgirls. The sun had come out and dried the fallen leaves, which crunched under our feet on the footpath. I wanted to sing suddenly, to ruffle my skirts and do one of our gypsy dances, full of passion and energy and rhythm. But there were other people on the path, walking with their dogs and kids on this fine autumn afternoon. They were mostly polite and some smiled at us, but I didn't really think they would understand if I'd launched into a gypsy dance.

five

I wore my uniform to school Monday morning, feeling like a million dollars, as they say on the movies. It was all I'd hoped and more. Dressed like everyone else, I suddenly became invisible. I could hold up my head and the sick scary feeling was gone from my stomach. Now that I wasn't watching out from the corner of my eye every moment, I could give all my attention to my school work. It was wonderful.

At dinner time, Rachel beckoned me over to the table the other girls were sharing. They were all excited about the weekend just past.

"You look so nice," said Chloe, and I knew that I did. My aunt had washed my hair and brushed it carefully, and the girl who looked back at me from the mirror in the girls' cloakroom had a new confidence that changed her whole appearance. I was pretty.

"Why don't you come to Beech Bank with us after school this afternoon?" Amber asked me.

I didn't understand. "Beech Bank? What is that?"

They explained that it was a club for kids to go after school, a place run by the local church. I did not quite understand. Our people do not have much to do with churches. I had been inside our village one a few times, out of curiosity, slipping in at the back and listening to the priest intoning his words to the worshippers, mostly old women in black head scarves. The air was heavy with incense and at one side was the figure of a man nailed to a cross by his hands and feet. It made me shudder, the dimness, the choking sweetness, the dying man. I was glad to get back to our cluttered noisy courtyard and the freshness of the lilac tree beside the well.

I said quickly, "I would not be allowed. My uncle would expect me to be there when he gets home. I have to help my aunt and do my school work for next day."

They looked disappointed. Then Chloe said, "We often do our homework at BB, there's a quiet room for it. Wouldn't they just let you do that?"

"Maybe I could ask my aunt," I said. "For tomorrow, but today I must go home."

Aunt Isabel thought it would be all right, as long as I was doing homework and not more than an hour late home. My aunt was proving wonderfully supportive of my attempts to fit into a different way of life.

"If only I had had these chances," she sighed, when we were together one evening. "I have so often longed for something more than endless work day after day, always at the beck and call of others. You must grasp every opportunity that comes, Madalina. And tell me all that you do, and how people live here, their homes, their families . . ."

She was echoing what my mother had said to me. They were helping me to experience a life they had never known themselves. And my aunt was hoping that in a small way she would be able to share those experiences with me. I gave her a hug, and promised I would tell her everything.

I don't know what I expected at the Beech Bank Club, but nothing like the way it turned out to be. Maybe I had a picture in my mind of dimness, of mustiness, a closed-in feeling, muttering old people and the image of a dying man. What I walked into was like an explosion of brightness and light. A place with many rooms running into each other, all painted in bright colours, small tables with red-patterned tablecloths, curtains at the big windows, games and books, music, the smell of coffee, comfortable chairs. And movement and sound, some people my age hurrying about, playing games, chattering, laughing, but others sitting quietly and talking or working on computers. The atmosphere was light too – light and free. People smiled at me and nobody stared or sneered or sniggered. It took my breath away.

Willow took my arm and steered me into the quiet area. "We'll get homework out of the way and then grab some coffee. Well, what do you think?"

I hardly knew what to think. I opened and closed my mouth a few times, and then all I could say was, "It doesn't look like a church!"

Willow laughed. "It is, though. Look up the word 'church' in the dictionary. It's not just a building. It's a gathering together of people."

My homework was soon done, and instead of taking the opportunity to read while I was waiting for the others to finish, I sat drinking it all in – the coffee mugs on the counter, shiny red and yellow with white dots, the smooth red metal of the café chairs, the click of ball against cue from the pool room next door. So different from the leisure room at the camp, with its fog of cigarette smoke and young men with a pool cue in one hand and a vodka bottle in the other, dirty jokes being exchanged. Uncle and Aunt had forbidden me to go there on my own. I wished they could see how different this place was.

Then I jumped a little as a man came over, pulled up

a chair and sat down near me. He looked friendly, was wearing jeans and a T-shirt and said, "Hi there. You must be Madalina."

I nodded and edged away a little. I didn't trust men, either my own countrymen or the ones here. My family had drummed it into me that nearly all men, except of course my family and the ones I knew, were probably out to take advantage of young girls and never to be trusted. I had every reason to believe them: once, returning from the shower block at the camp at nightfall, I had been waylaid and grabbed at by one of the vodka-drinking youths. My nimble footwork had kept me safe, but now I always made sure that Aunt Isabel and I went together to the facilities. I was beginning to see why my uncle and even the Gangmaster found me such a responsibility.

This man held out his hand, and said, "I'm Rod. Nice to meet you." I shook his hand as quickly as I could. Amber came over then, to my great relief, and then Annie, and they both chatted to Rod, mostly about things that had happened over the weekend. I couldn't follow everything that was said, but it seemed they'd had an exciting time. They tried to include me in the conversation, but I kept my head down and didn't say much. When the man moved on to another group, Willow looked at me and said, "That's Rod, our vicar."

"Vicar? You mean – like a priest?"

"Yes, much the same. He and his wife run this place."

I was amazed. "But – but he was not wearing black! He seemed just like an ordinary man!"

She laughed. "He *is* an ordinary man."

"An ordinary ordained man," said Chloe, and they both laughed again, but not in a sneery way, and not at me. I relaxed again. There was a silvery metal clock on the wall, and I saw that my time was almost up. I'd have to hurry to get home along the footpath before my uncle got back from work. I sighed, and noticed a cross on the wall just opposite the clock, but this cross was empty and had no dying man nailed to it. I wondered what it meant, and what the church was all about. There were questions buzzing round in my head.

But they'd all have to wait. "I must go," I told the others with real regret.

"Me too. I'll walk with you as far as the end of my lane," said Rachel.

We left the others and set off. Rachel is a talkative person and chattered on about this and that as we walked. There were things that I'd have liked to ask, but for now I had this deep contentment, a sense of belonging that was new and satisfying and comforting. It wasn't just the school uniform. It was the feeling that I had friends, people who liked me and accepted me and wanted to be with me and share with me. For the very first time in my life, I understood what a friend is.

PART FIVE

Willow's Story

ALL CHANGE

one

That Friday night at Beech Bank was a real turning point for me. I knew as I left there that my life had changed, permanently. There was the challenge of the Mission presentation. And there was Jay.

Walking home, I tried to tone down the girls' teasing remarks. They were all hyped up, on a great big high. I was trying desperately to keep some kind of order, in my own thoughts as much as anything. And to get them off the subject of Jay until I had thought it through for myself. So it was a great relief when Chloe came up with the idea of school uniform for Madalina, and they all picked up on it. It was a brilliant idea, I had to admit, and we discussed how it could be done until we parted company. We'd meet at my house tomorrow. And we'd pray for a way to approach Madalina. Maybe I'd better be the one to say something to her, I thought.

"Control freak!" said Rachel.

For some reason, that remark stuck in my mind when we'd gone our separate ways. For a little while it even blotted out the other thoughts that filled my mind. I knew Rachel was only teasing, they'd been doing that since we left Beech Bank. She and I have been mates since nursery school and we love each other to bits. I know she has this habit of blurting out the first thing that comes into her head and sometimes regretting it. It didn't mean a thing.

But was I a control freak? Maybe there was some truth in what she'd said. Certainly for most of my childhood I'd longed for some kind of control. Not that my parents were bad. Just different. They loved me and my brother Rowan but our lives were not like other kids' lives. Other kids' dads didn't have ponytails (thankfully he'd cut it off now) and lead protest demos, other kids' mums weren't artists who forgot everything when they were working – forgot to eat or sleep, or clean the house, or that they had appointments or even probably that they had kids! (Maybe that bit is an exaggeration, to be fair.) Other families didn't fancy themselves to be eco-warriors, camping out in the big gas pipeline that went through this area a few years ago. They didn't have messy homes and hippie clothes and have to eat organic food when what they really longed for was a McDonald's burger and a big ice-cream dessert with loads of sauce laden with E-numbers. Maybe this was why I had my room all pristine and tasteful, why I spent my hard-earned money on co-ordinated designer clothes and accessories, instead of cheap and cheerful High Street stuff or hippie gear. Why I liked to organise and lead and guide people. But I wasn't controlling. Was I?

I hoped not. Anyway, by the time I reached home I'd stopped trying to puzzle it out and let my mind go back to where it really wanted to be – that meeting with Jay. He'd stood out immediately from the others on stage, and not just his looks. His personality came over, strong and determined. I was moved to tears by the film, like the others, and a bit disorientated when it ended. Everyone was moving around, talking and drifting towards the buffet tables, when I heard this voice behind me.

"Hey there!"

My heart skipped a beat. It was him, Jay, even taller and better-looking close up. And he was speaking to me!

"Oh – hello." I'm not normally at a loss for words, but suddenly I felt quite tongue-tied and flustered. I had a horrid feeling that I was going to blush, which I don't do often, but which is disastrous teamed with my red hair. I collected my wits and felt the blush subside, to my great relief.

He stuck out his hand and said, "I'm Jay. And you are . . .?"

"Willow," I said, wondering if he'd think it a weird name. Most American girls seem to be called cute names like Sammy Jo or Brandilyn. But he smiled and said, "Suits you. Willowy. Graceful."

I smiled and said thank you, and hoped I wasn't simpering, whatever simpering is. I was so glad I was wearing my newest jeans and tunic top, with a little discreet jewellery. Jay's eyes were even bluer close up, and when he smiled he had the most perfect white teeth. He didn't have a crew cut like I imagined most American boys have, but neatly-trimmed hair with a bit that flopped forward over his forehead, like Robert Redford in some oldie films I've seen.

"What did you think of the movie presentation?" he asked.

I checked an impulse to begin gushing about how wonderful and touching it had been. I paused for a moment and then said, "It was very challenging. Emotive, but I guess we have to step back and think clearly and carefully about what can be done."

I was rather proud of that little speech. He liked it too. "That's what I felt when I first got into this. First impulse is to jump right in, volunteer, join up for *something*. But these projects are not to be entered lightly. Lots of prayer and preparation needed."

I nodded, and he said, "I guess you're one of the leaders here?"

I was a bit startled by this, and found myself saying, "Well, kind of. I lead a class some of the time."

"Thought so. I lead a Sunday School class back home."

And then he began telling me about where he lived in the States, his church, his studies, and his family – his "folks" as he called them. And asked about mine. Then suddenly he paused, glanced across the room and said, "Hey Willow, I think someone's trying to get your attention. Some girls from your Bible class, maybe?"

I looked across and there were the others, all agog, giggling, waving and no doubt making silly remarks. I'd have to go and join them. "Oh yes. Please excuse me," I said, and he said, "Sure. Don't let me keep you. Maybe see you in church on Sunday? A couple of us are staying over at the Vicarage."

My heart leapt. I couldn't wait to see him again. But I had this odd little nagging uncomfortable feeling as I went across to join the others. I realised, with a strange mixture of dismay and gratification, that he believed I was older than I was, maybe 17 or 18, his age. And I'd made no attempt at all to set him straight.

Anyway, I hadn't deliberately misled him, I told myself as I reached home. Rowan was in bed, Mum and Dad were watching some documentary on global warming, I could hear it from the hallway. Mum called out to me, "Hey, honey, come and watch this – you'd find it interesting."

The thing is, I probably would. I was concerned about a lot of the same things as they were, a lot of the time, and I felt the same way as they did about saving the planet and caring for the environment and the people in it. It was only so often, out of sheer perversity I suppose, that I felt like going out, eating a whole lot of junk food and then throwing the polystyrene wrapping into the river! I didn't do that, of course, and I was gradually growing out of that teenage contrariness. I knew they'd want to discuss the programme afterwards, and I wanted to be alone with my thoughts. So I called back, "Going to have a bath, Mum, and then going to bed."

Going into my room always feels like entering a lovely, peaceful, private, ordered haven. Ideally, I'd have an en-suite to go with it, all gleaming chrome and pristine tiles. In actual fact, I had to go across the landing to the family bathroom, with a chip in the handbasin and discarded underwear and wet towels left on the floor by Rowan. I picked them up between finger and thumb and dropped them in the laundry basket while the bathtub filled. I poured in bubble-bath and climbed in to soak in the bubbles and think some more about the evening. I deliberately switched my mind back to the conversation we'd had on the way home. Chloe had the idea about school uniform for Madalina and we'd all caught on. It might be just what she needed. I remembered I'd got an unopened pack of two white school shirts, and I was sure there was a new pack of black socks too. They could be my contribution. I also thought of the warm quilted black jacket in my wardrobe, a really nice one and just the thing for winter. I really liked it, but, hey, I had no shortage of jackets and it would look great on Madalina.

I concentrated hard on our plan, and on meeting the girls tomorrow. But all the time a pair of blue eyes and blonde floppy hair would keep intruding into my thoughts. I was surprised at myself. I never remembered feeling this way before.

The water was cooling and I turned on the hot tap to top it up. The plumbing in our house is ancient, and when the hot tap runs the pipes clank and rattle. A few minutes later there were footsteps on the stairs and a knock on the door. Dad's voice said, "Hey, Willow, don't use up all the hot water! Leave some for the rest of us!"

I sighed and turned off the tap. He went downstairs, but a moment later there were bare feet padding along the landing and Rowan's sleepy voice saying, "Willow, are you in there? Hurry up, I want to go to the toilet."

I sighed again, wallowed my way out of the bubbles and reached for a towel. Control freak or not, I have no chance of controlling anything that goes on in this house.

two

I always thought I had my life well sussed out. It was a revelation to me, after I became a Christian and started studying the Bible, to find that God has a plan for each and every one of us, a kind of blueprint all set out. Of course, we have the choice and it's up to us whether we choose to fit into it or not. At first, I was afraid God's plan for me might involve something really hard and difficult, or dull and boring, but after talking with Rod and Sadie I began to see that God has given us each our gifts and interests and passions, to get us ready and prepared to fit in with his plans.

It all became much clearer. For example, Chloe has always wanted to be a writer and that's something God has given her and wants her to use. He'd be unlikely, for instance, to ask her to be a deep-sea diver or an engineer when all she wants is to be writing stuff. Me,

I've always been keen on dress design, textiles and the fashion industry. I thought about a modelling career for a while, being tall and skinny and having what our art teacher calls "titian" hair. But strutting a catwalk didn't really appeal to me. What I really fancied was working with beautiful materials and being involved with designing beautiful clothes. I was sure I could make a go of it. Good grades at A level, then a degree in textile design, then design work, and maybe my own fashion house! I'd already chosen my GCSE options and was working hard.

Now, all of a sudden, I wasn't so sure. I'd thought God was leading me along this pathway but now I had doubts. Since that evening at Beech Bank, I looked at the open doors of my clothes cupboards with new eyes. Usually it gave me a big kick – row upon row of colour-co-ordinated, good quality, beautiful designer clothes – but now I felt something that was almost like shame. Madalina's mouth had dropped open in surprise when she saw them. She had gasped something about a wonderful boutique. Her clothes would probably fit into a tiny corner of my cupboard space. And as for the African kids in the film – well, what they had was practically zilch. For the first time I really questioned what I was doing with all this stuff.

I really needed to talk it all over with someone, and the first thing that came into my head was that I'd like to talk to Jay about it. I mentally kicked myself for being so stupid. I'd only met Jay once and chatted to him for about five minutes, for goodness sake! What on earth could I be thinking! Sadie or Rod, or the other girls, were the obvious ones to discuss my ideas with. Or even Mum and Dad!

But already my mind was running ahead. Maybe I could sell most of the stuff in my wardrobe, on eBay or something. The money could go towards the costs for my mission project. And I'd put the money I earned babysitting, and dog walking, and shopping for old folks, towards that too: the money I usually spent on the latest brand names.

In the meantime, Jay was here for another few days and I'd be seeing him again! The thought made my heart give a little skip and jump! I hurried through my Saturday morning trip to the Co-op, shopping for a pair of pensioners, and decided to mosey round the Saturday market. Rachel and Annie turned up there too. Possibly, I thought, Jay would be out exploring the town; Americans liked quaint country towns with the odd cobbled street, didn't they? We might just bump into him. I didn't mention this to the others though. I'd never have heard the last of it.

We didn't see Jay, but we did bump into Madalina and her aunt, and realised that the school uniform plan could go into operation right now. We'd discussed it earlier, and it only took a few minutes to get Amber and Chloe round to mine too with their contributions. Madalina seemed quite overwhelmed, but in a happy way. It was all very satisfying, and I was glad we'd done it.

Sunday morning seemed a long time coming that

week, but it was here at last. All five of us girls turned up for morning worship, you can bet nobody wanted to miss out on anything. And there they were, Jay and the other two, Matt and Ed, up at the front with Rod, checking out the service programme. I saw Jay's blonde head turn and see us, he smiled and waved and my heart flipped again. This wasn't lost on the other girls, of course.

"I reckon he's going to ask you out, Wills," said Rachel, in far too loud a stage whisper for my liking. "I feel it in my bones!"

"Don't be ridiculous," I hissed, feeling the colour coming into my face.

"I hope you'll be keeping your mind on the sermon, my dear," said Amber in prim schoolteacherish tones.

"Remember we're in church," added Chloe. I had the horrid feeling that they were getting their own back for the way I sometimes talked to them. All of them were giggling fit to bust. They can be so immature at times! I sincerely hoped that Jay would get no inkling of all this, or that if he did, he would realise that I for one had left behind such childish behaviour long ago.

I also hoped I wasn't showing any of the confusion I felt inside, although the other girls were not exactly helping. I'd never in my life felt this way about any boy before. The ones my own age seemed little more than children. Suddenly, this person was of the utmost importance to me. I couldn't understand it at all. I couldn't have fallen in love, could I?

I tried my hardest to keep my mind on the service, and the words we were speaking and singing, and the worship, but I had a hard job of it, with the back of Jay's head directly in my line of vision at the front of the church, and then his face when he and the others stood up and shared a little about themselves and their work, as they'd done at Beech Bank. Afterwards I just wanted to get home asap. He's not really interested, I told myself firmly. He'll probably hardly speak to me, or just very casually.

I'd pretty well convinced myself, and was heading towards the door when I heard his voice above the general chatter.

"Willow! Hey, hang on just a mo!"

He politely made his way through the people, saying, "Excuse me, ma'am," and, "Excuse me, sir," until he reached me. He really was good-looking, with that lock of hair flopping over his forehead and the sweetest smile. He said, "I wondered if we could meet up later. Go for a walk or something. You could show me the neighbourhood."

Well, what could I say, when my heart was leaping, and I was inwardly saying "Yes! Yes!" What I did say, in a voice that came out surprisingly calm and casual, was, "OK then, that would be cool. How about 2.30 at the end of the bridge?"

He nodded, and was immediately grabbed by someone wanting to shake his hand. I joined the others, trying to look nonchalant. They were fairly bursting with suppressed excitement.

"What did I tell you?" said Rachel, with a glint of triumph in her eye.

three

I spent ages trying to decide what to wear that afternoon, pulling out half a dozen outfits and piling them on the bed. Once again, I was struck by the sheer volume of the clothes I owned. Some items I'd never even worn, some only once or twice. Something would have to be done about reducing my wardrobe, drastically.

I just couldn't decide whether to keep on the clothes I'd worn to church, maybe just changing out of my good leather boots into something suitable for walking. Would it look obvious if I got all dolled up from scratch again? Should I just settle for something casual?

In the end I did the latter, changing into jeans, a zipped hoodie, and trainers. I'd told my parents at lunch I was going for a walk with someone from church, though I didn't say it was an American lad four years older than myself who I'd just met. Not that they'd make a fuss, they do trust me to be sensible. And I am. Usually. At the moment, though, my wits seemed to have flown out the window.

Next I agonised over what time I should reach the bridge. Too early, and I'd look over eager. On the dot would give the impression of being a regimented, inflexible kind of person. In the end, I dithered so long that it was already twenty-five to three when I left the house. And then I fretted in case he'd got fed up of waiting or think I hadn't meant it. Whatever had happened to cool, controlled, disciplined and unflappable Willow?

I needn't have worried, because he was there, leaning over the bridge and snapping views of the river with a digital camera. He turned as I came up and his face lit up with that wonderful smile. "Hey there! You made it!"

I didn't like to point out that I only live three streets away, which doesn't require too much effort. I said, "Shall we go along the river walk?"

"Whatever you say! You're the neighbourhood expert!"

We went through the little gate and down to the pathway beside the old railway track. I skidded a little on damp leaves, and Jay put out a hand to steady me. It gave me a warm kind of feeling – I don't bring out a protective instinct in people usually.

"Tell me more about your family," I asked, for the sake of something to say.

"Sure." He paused for a moment and fumbled in one of the big pockets of his jacket, producing a photo from a wallet. He handed it to me. I saw a family grouped around a wrought-iron seat on a green lawn – mum and dad sitting with the smallest child, a little girl, between them, another girl, about my age, perched on one of the arms, three boys standing behind. The one in the middle and the tallest of them was Jay. All of the children had a strong family resemblance, blonde hair and big smiles. Behind them was a long, white house with a veranda running right across the front and a flight of steps flanked by pillars and flowering shrubs. I thought, goodness, they must be loaded to live in a place like that! Maybe Jay's dad owns a whole chain of hardware stores.

I hoped I wasn't gawping like an idiot, and said, "Wow! What a beautiful place! And a lovely family. Are you the oldest?"

"Yeah. They're great. I miss them loads. Can't wait to see them."

He put the photo away and we set off along the path, footsteps muffled by fallen leaves. Every so often Jay stopped, aimed his camera and took a picture of something – a leafless twig against the greyish river water, a spray of elderberries, a yellow leaf, even a close-up of the silvery trunk of a birch.

"You like photography?" I asked.

He snapped another pic of fallen leaves around the trunk of an oak. "Yeah, but it's the trees I'm really into. I love 'em. Always have, even in winter when the leaves are off and you can really see the shapes of the branches and twigs. The colours are great here. I've been up to New England couple of times, just to see the fall colours. You should see the red maples! Some people chase around from place to place all fall, just catching the best of the colours. Leaf-peepers, they call them."

He aimed and clicked again. "I was seriously thinking

of a career with trees, until this mission chance came up," he said. "Maybe I'll still be able to work with trees in some way. Tree-planting programmes in deforested areas, or something, combined with mission work." His eyes were bright and he seemed all lit up from inside. I knew the feeling. I'd already learned that God often uses us in areas we're passionate about. I was pondering this when Jay stopped suddenly. "Willow, quick! Stand up there on that bank – just there, by the beech tree."

I had no idea what he was getting at. Had he seen a snake or something? We do get adders along there sometimes, but usually when it's warm and sunny.

"I want to get a pic of you," he explained. "Just there, in that patch of sunlight. I want it to catch your hair, with the beech leaves behind."

A ray of sunlight had broken through the grey clouds, dappling the fallen leaves and lighting up the beech tree. He grinned with satisfaction when he had clicked the picture and looked at it. He showed it to me – my hair and the beech leaves gleaming russet with the sun on them.

"Willow, the Beech Bank girl!" he said. "You know, you look about 12 in that picture."

I felt the smile fade from my face. I still hadn't mentioned my real age. I'd have to come clean. I said quickly, not giving myself a chance to chicken out, "Jay, there's something I have to tell you." He looked at me expectantly, eyebrows raised. "It's just – well, I have the feeling you think I'm your age. Well, I'm not. I'm the same age as the other girls. I'm 14. And a week." I wished I hadn't added that last bit, it's the kind of thing little kids say.

He didn't say anything for a moment. I sneaked a glance at him and he was looking a bit nonplussed. My heart sank. I didn't think he'd really want to know me now. Then he said, slowly, "That does surprise me. I did think you were around my age. You seem a lot older than 14, really mature. But it's OK. It's cool. In fact . . ." He paused, then went on: "I have something to confess too. You thought that place in the picture was my home, right?"

I nodded, surprised. "Isn't it?"

He shook his head. "No, our place is just a regular house, nothing fancy. That place in the photo is where people in our neighbourhood go to get their pictures taken. Makes a nice backdrop. Actually, it's the public library."

I couldn't help it, I just caught his eye and burst out laughing. There we both were, laughing our heads off, with the river glugging by and leaves falling as the sun went in and a breeze picked up.

"There's another thing," he said. "My name isn't really Jay. It's James Dean Anderson. My mom had this thing about old movie stars. We're all named after them. My brothers are Spencer Tracey and Kirk Douglas, my older sister is Judy Garland and my little sister is Grace Kelly. You can bet we all shortened them pretty soon. I was called JD for ages, then it got shortened to just Jay."

"I like it," I said. "Anything else to confess?"

"No, that's it. You?" I shook my head, we laughed

again, and I suddenly felt light and free, and not at all bothered about the impression I was making or what he was thinking of me. We walked on along the river bank, chatting about families, homes, trees, school, work, music bands and everything under the sun, like a pair of old friends. Coming up the lane that linked the river path to the town, I had a sense of deep contentment, that all was well with my world. I remembered something I'd read – written by an old hermit woman called Julian of Norwich, I think – *"All shall be well, and all shall be most well, and all manner of things shall be well."* Or something like that. Anyway, it was how I was feeling.

The short afternoon was beginning to close in, the sun had dropped out of sight and lights were beginning to twinkle all over the town.

"I'll walk you home," said Jay, and I didn't even give a thought to what he might make of our messy disorganised house and my hippy-dippy parents. It didn't seem to matter a bit.

four

Of course, the girls made a big deal of it at school next day. They expected a blow-by-blow account of the whole afternoon. I told them we'd walked along the river path and taken lots of photos of trees. They seemed disappointed.

"And did he – er – kiss you?" Rachel ventured to ask.

"No, he didn't."

"Did you hold hands?"

"No, we didn't."

"Well, what *happened* then?"

"I told you. We walked and talked and took pictures."

What did they expect, for goodness sake, a mad snogging session among the hollies and hazels? They really do need to grow up a little!

"And are you seeing him again?"

"Yes, he'll be at BB this afternoon I expect, then he and Matt and Ed are leaving Tuesday morning. Maybe we'll email."

"And that's it then? No big romance?"

"No big romance." I smiled at their disappointed faces. Nothing could ruffle the sense of peace and quiet contentment that was still with me. I didn't know what might happen in the future, but for now, Jay and I were friends and we would both trust God to lead us in the way that we should go. Madalina was in school wearing her new uniform and looking like a different girl. We were really making a difference in her life, and she was planning to come to BB later this week. Everything was right with my world.

Until the afternoon, that is. We were changing after netball, which we'd shared with the Year Eleven girls. Being tall, I'm good at scoring and I'd done well that afternoon. I was fastening my shoes when Melanie Fisher came sauntering over. "Hey there, Willow. Good game."

"Thanks," I said, surprised. Melanie Fisher doesn't normally give me the time of day. She's not a bad player, but away from netball we don't mix much. Now she seemed to want to stop and chat.

"Saw you yesterday afternoon," she remarked casually. "Just coming up from the river path. Nice fella."

Ah, so that was it! I had to admit I'd been so absorbed I hadn't noticed who was about yesterday. Trust Melanie to notice. She has strong radar where the male sex is concerned.

"New boyfriend?" she asked, leaning against the next locker and twirling a strand of blonde hair around a finger.

"Not really. Just a friend. He came with a group to Beech Bank last Friday."

She looked thoughtful. "Oh, I see. That's the church thing in the old community centre, isn't it? Can anyone go?"

Uh–oh! My heart sank. I knew what was coming. I nodded, and she said, still casual, "Maybe I'll check it out then after school. See ya!"

And off she sauntered, all voluptuous curves and blonde hair.

I put my head in my hands.

"What was all that about?" asked Amber, who'd heard the last bit.

"Don't ask! Just Melanie being Melanie! Saw me with Jay yesterday and now she's decided to come to BB."

Amber whistled through her teeth. "Whew! She really

is a piece of work, isn't she? Thinks she's irresistible. Usually is too, as far as the dorky lads round here go. Bet she'll come with her shirt buttons undone a couple more notches, and be all over Jay and Ed and Matt like a rash."

"I think they'll have enough sense to see through her," I said, trying to convince myself. But inwardly I wasn't so sure. Some men are, after all, easily swayed by wide eyes and batting eyelashes, never mind Melanie's other attributes. I didn't want her to go to Beech Bank and get talking to Jay. Suddenly I wasn't so cool after all, in fact I wasn't cool at all when I thought of Jay being chatted up by someone else. My bubble had well and truly burst.

The other girls were sympathetic. Going to the next class, Rachel said, "Shall I tell her she wouldn't fit in at BB, warn her off?"

"We can't do that," I said. "We're supposed to welcome everyone who wants to come. We can't pick and choose. We spent all lunchtime trying to get Madalina to come, didn't we?"

"Yes, but Melanie only wants to flirt," said Chloe. "She's coming for the wrong reasons."

"We ought to be praying," said Annie, and I knew she was right.

"But how? Should we pray that she sprains her ankle or something, or develops an allergy to that fish we had for lunch and comes out in a horrible spotty rash?" said Rachel, half joking.

I was almost ready to pray along those lines myself.

But some words from the Bible came into my mind: *"Be kind and compassionate to one another, forgiving each other, just as in Christ God forgave you."*

Just as we were going into class, Annie paused at the door and said thoughtfully, "I think we ought to ask God to work things out the way he thinks best."

She was right, of course. Annie is getting to be very wise, in spite of the fact that she's only just getting to know the Lord.

I prayed quietly in my heart as we settled down for English Lit, and some of the horrid sick feeling lifted a little.

When we reached Beech Bank later, Jay and the two others were there, chatting to Rod and Hugh as they got the games area sorted. Jay waved and grinned when he saw me and said he'd see me later. He had on a blue shirt the exact colour of his eyes. Other kids were coming in, but no sign of Melanie. Maybe she'd thought better of it after all. But she hadn't. She arrived twenty-five minutes later, having evidently been home to change into a mini-skirt and tight sweater which left nothing to the imagination and put the rest of us at a disadvantage, still in our school uniform.

"Talk about obvious!" muttered Amber.

I sighed. Everything seemed to have gone pear-shaped, I thought, and that's a fact and not a comment on Melanie's figure! Sure enough, she homed in on the three lads like a ferret after a rabbit, introducing herself and chatting animatedly. They seemed to be nothing loath, even enjoying the talk and having a laugh. Jay's lock of hair flopped over his forehead, and I felt that for two pins Melanie would reach up and smooth it back. If she does that, I thought, I will scream! I will definitely scream!

She didn't, but there seemed to be a lot of joking and laughing going on in that quarter. I got a coffee and sat at one of the small tables, stirring it gloomily and reflecting on the way things can change from day to day, or even hour to hour. Annie and Chloe were doing homework, Rachel and Amber batting a table tennis ball around. Not even Sadie was there to talk to, it must be her turn to stay in with the babies.

I was almost deciding that I might as well call it a day and go home, when a shadow fell across the table and Jay was pulling out the chair opposite and sitting down. "Hey! At last!" He sighed with something that seemed like relief. "Thought I'd never get the chance to catch up."

"You seemed to be having a good time," I said, before I could stop myself. I'm not normally given to bitchy remarks, but Jay didn't seem to notice anyway.

"Yeah, well, it can get to be a strain being polite to everyone, but you have to try, I guess," he said. "Do you know that girl, Melissa, is it?"

"Melanie. Not very well. She's at my school," I said.

"She has problems, I'd say," he said, wrinkling his forehead.

"Really?" And I bet she loved telling them to you, I thought meanly.

"Yeah. Attention seeking. Serious insecurity, I would

think. And have you heard her laugh? Man, it cuts like a knife!"

Suddenly I heard the laugh, resounding across the room from where she was still chatting to Matt and Ed, high and a little screechy, like a knife against metal. Strange I'd never noticed it before. Jay winced. "Poor girl. I hope she'll be able to find what she's looking for here. Maybe you can help her."

Looking into his sky-blue eyes, I knew that he was quite sincere.

"Maybe we can," I said, and meant it.

Jay smiled. "Meantime, I could do with a coffee. Do you want another? Rod asked me to do an epilogue later, and I'd like your ideas."

"Yes please," I said, and smiled back, and suddenly I felt warm and peaceful again, and knew that Annie's prayer had been the right one.

five

So that was it then. Jay, Matt and Ed left on the Tuesday morning and everything settled back to normal again. Except that it wasn't. Over the space of four or five days, less than a week, I felt that my life had changed in many ways.

Meeting Jay for one, of course. He had burst into my carefully controlled and ordered life and turned it all upside down. Kind of. Because out of all the stomach-churning, heart-fluttering confusion of love at first sight (which I only admitted to myself, and which I wasn't sure about anyway), had come something that I knew was going to be lasting and good, maybe not romantic love at all, but something that would endure and grow and would go on for our lifetimes. I don't know how I knew it, but I did.

And then there was the challenge of the Aid Mission movie and the possibilities it had thrown up. It had made me seriously question the way I'd been planning my life. Suddenly my dreams seemed so self-centred. Yes, God had given me talents and interests to develop and use. But maybe they'd be used in other ways than I'd thought. Jay felt that his passion for trees could perhaps be used in the re-planting of deforested areas. Maybe my love for textiles and design could be involved with producing clothing that would do away with child labour and pitifully small wages. How this could work I didn't have a clue. But God had his own plan for my life, and it would be the most exciting adventure ever to discover it and fit into it a bit at a time. I could make a difference, I really could. Already we were making a difference to Madalina, and it was fantastic to see her joining in and laughing and enjoying life here. I even felt different towards Melanie Fisher, seeing a little of what Jay had seen, that the posing and flirting was a desperate bid for attention which probably covered a real insecurity and unhappiness. If she turned up at Beech Bank again, I really would try to help her.

In the meantime, I was going to get started on the reducing of my wardrobe to an acceptable level. Opening the cupboard doors on the day after Jay left (oh dear, I even seem to be recording time now as Before Jay and After Jay!), I was gobsmacked again at the amount of stuff I possessed. Almost obscene, I thought. I'd earned the money for almost everything, and not all of it was new; it's amazing what bargains you can pick up if you really search at charity shops and boot sales. But it all had to be immaculate and designer labelled. I'd been obsessed with brand names and labels. I'd heard about shopping addiction, and I wondered for the first time if that's what I'd had. Anyway, I was going to do something about it. It was something else that was going to change.

I mentioned this at school next day. The others looked at me in astonishment.

"You mean, get rid of all your beautiful clothes?"

"Well, I'll keep some, obviously," I said. "But I don't need half that stuff. Don't even wear some of it, or ever likely to."

"But you love your clothes!"

This was true. I did love the look, the feel of the fabrics, the way things were cut and the way they hung. But all of a sudden I could see that I didn't need to *own* it all. And I suddenly realised that new things didn't really satisfy. I'd buy something gorgeous, hang it up, admire it, maybe wear it a time or two. And in a week or so I'd be wanting something else.

I tried to explain this. "It's like walking in some beautiful garden, seeing lovely flowers and shrubs, or looking at a lovely view. You should be able to enjoy things and appreciate them without wanting to have them for yourself."

I didn't think I was making my point very clearly, and neither did the girls. Amber and Rachel looked completely mystified and even Chloe was wrinkling her forehead.

"How are you going to do it?" asked Annie at last.

"Well . . ." This was what I'd been trying to work out. In a sudden flash of inspiration, I said, "For starters, I'd like all of you to choose one thing for yourself, whatever you like. Madalina too. By the way, where is Madalina?"

"She went to see Bogdan about something," said Rachel. "Do you really mean it, Wills? We can pick anything we like?"

"Yes." All of a sudden I felt like a real Lady Bountiful.

Amber's eyes gleamed. "Wow! I bags the Grace Ellen jacket, the green one."

"Could I have that cardigan/shrug thing with the fur bits?" asked Chloe.

"I was going to ask for that," said Amber. "But you have it. I could have that stripey top. Or the combats with silver bits. Unless you'd like them, Rach?"

"My legs are way too short," said Rachel ruefully. "But I'm sure I'll think of something else."

It gave me a funny sort of feeling, hearing them discussing and picking over my designer wardrobe like a crowd of old biddies at a jumble sale. But I'd made the decision and I was going through with it. And I'd just had an idea for what to do with the rest of my stuff. But there was no time to mention it now. The bell had just gone and we were heading for class.

At Beech Bank later I told the others my idea.

"I wondered if we could have a sale. Maybe here at Beech Bank. Exclusive designer items. We could borrow a garment rail and maybe get hold of a couple of dummies somewhere. Or maybe we could have a fashion show and invite other people."

The others seized on this at once.

"We could make a catwalk and model the clothes!" said Annie. "You know you'd make a great model, Wills!"

"We could all model in turns," said Amber.

"What, with my legs?"

"Yes, so that people can see you don't have to be tall and skinny to look good, that anyone can look like a million dollars."

"It could be an auction. That way we'd make more money."

"We could all contribute something. We've all got stuff we could do without."

"It would have to be good stuff though, like Willow's. No old tat."

"'Course not. Are you suggesting I wear old tat?"

"Nooooo, I was just saying!"

"What will we do with the money, anyway?"

They all looked at me. "I thought it could go towards the Aid Mission. Or towards our expenses for when we go ourselves," I said.

"Great idea! We could have chocolates to give out, and print programmes, and make a proper evening of it."

They were getting carried away again, and I was grateful for their enthusiasm. "Maybe we'd better talk it all over with Rod and Sadie," I said.

"Sadie could model for us!" said Chloe excitedly. "With her legs and cheekbones and all. You and her together, you'd be like Naomi Campbell and Kate Moss."

"Hardly," I said. But I was getting excited myself as I thought of the possibilities. We had already started making a difference for Madalina; it didn't have to stop there! Maybe we could ask Madalina to bring her aunt along, or some of the other migrant women. It could be like a first glimpse of real church for them. We could put up posters in town. Maybe decorate Beech Bank to look like a fashion salon. The sky was the limit, really.

It gave me a little pang to think of just a few clothes left hanging in my wardrobe. Would the rest be properly looked after by the people who bought them? I told myself that that wouldn't be my responsibility. I would just have to let them go.

For now, there was Beech Bank, and discussing the idea with Sadie, and then home, tea, homework, texting mates and checking my emails. My heart gave a leap. Maybe I'd check the emails first of all. There might just be one from Jay.

PART SIX

Amber's Story

SISTER ACT

one

I've always had a special love for animals, even before my elder brother Charlie decided to become a vet. And especially dogs. I really love dogs. I like their enthusiasm, intelligence, their single-mindedness, their energy and their loyalty. I love the way they look, bright eyes, flying ears, lolling tongues, big paws, or whatever else their particular breed might have in the way of striking features. My family always says that when me, my parents and little sister go out in the car, my dad notices the other cars on the road, my mum notices the people, and my little sister notices the babies in prams. I notice the dogs. It's true.

Dogs are actually more interesting than people, I find. I still miss Barney, my dog who was my age and who died a few weeks ago. I was heartbroken that I didn't get the chance to say goodbye to him, and that I didn't even know he was being put to sleep until afterwards.

But that's all water under the bridge now. Now we have Hamlet, who I've bonded with as I feel I understand him best. Hamlet may have his particular problems, and the other girls are sometimes quite rude about him, but I know that what he needs is lots and lots of TLC. Not every dog has to be big and butch.

There were several interesting things that came out of that day when Willow, Chloe, Hamlet and I hiked up to the migrant camp. To begin with, we got a glimpse of how Madalina lives, and since then we've got to know Madalina herself a lot better, and hopefully helped her a bit. It must be hard to have almost nothing, like her family. And to be so bright and yet not be able to have the chance to learn properly. Although in some ways her life as a gypsy in Romania sounds really dramatic and colourful. She did a dance for us at school the other day and it was amazing! Just made us all want to get up and dance and whirl ourselves. But we were getting changed for gym at the time, and Miss Pierce came in and told us to stop stomping about and get downstairs, pronto! However, at the next break, Miss Pierce, who teaches drama as well, nobbled Madalina between classes.

"As some of us seem so keen to learn Romanian gypsy dancing, would you be prepared to give some lessons to the class? Maybe we could do a study on your culture?"

Madalina looked nervous again, and glanced at me and Chloe, who happened to be walking with her. She said "I . . . I am not sure. What would I have to do?"

"Just teach us the moves to some of your traditional dances. I'm sure we can track down some appropriate music."

I liked the sound of this. All that stamping and clapping and twirling sounded like good fun, better than Shakespeare sonnets anyway. Maybe we'd get to wear costumes, those long flouncy skirts with bells and things. I nudged Madalina and hissed, "Say you'll do it, Madalina! It'll be fun!"

She still looked very doubtful, but nodded, and said, "Yes, I will do it," and Miss Pierce looked pleased and said, "Good! I'll look into appropriate music and read up on the culture. It'll be good for everyone."

I wondered if she and the other teaching staff knew about some of the snide, subtle bullying that went on. Maybe educating the kids about cultures and traditions would do more than all the lengthy lectures and punishments they used to try and control bullying. Good old Miss Pierce. And good old Madalina for agreeing. I gave her a congratulatory high five as we went into class, though she still looked a bit scared.

"It'll be fun!" I said again. She didn't look totally convinced.

To be honest, I was absolutely fascinated by Madalina and the glimpse of her life we'd had that day at the migrant camp. Willow and Chloe had really bent my ear about running across there with Hamlet and talking to strange men, but I'd do it again for two pins. Madalina's uncle may have seemed strange and scary that day, but from what she said about him, he's basically a kind and caring man, though wary of life in a strange place and inclined to be over-protective of his family. Just like my dad, in fact. I'd have loved a chance to talk to him more, because what interested me most was the way he communicated with his dog, the one that almost scared poor little Hamlet out of his wits. I'd asked Madalina about it, but she couldn't really explain.

"He just does it. He has the gift."

"But *how?* How does he train the dogs to understand?"

"Train them?"

"Yes. Teach them, you know, like, to do what he wants."

"He doesn't do that. They just understand him. He's always done it. Many of us do. With horses, too."

"Like that film, *The Horse Whisperer*," said Rachel.

Madalina looked mystified. She hadn't seen the film. But I was getting more and more intrigued. I'd love to speak again to her uncle, to learn something of this gift of communication with animals that he possessed.

Unfortunately, I made the mistake of mentioning all this at home. My dad went ballistic when he heard I'd actually been to the migrant camp.

"You *what?* You went to one of those camps and got mixed up with foreign workers?"

"I didn't get mixed up with them," I said. "Well, at least, Hamlet did nearly get mixed up with one of their dogs. It was by accident. But that's what I'm saying. This man could control the dog without saying a word or doing anything, just making this weird whispery clicking sound."

I was digging myself in deeper and deeper, and Dad was not impressed. "You mean to say there was a dog fight, and a weird man – what in the world have you been getting into?"

"The *man* wasn't weird. He's Madalina's uncle, and he's really nice, and he has this gift . . ."

But Dad wasn't listening. He turned to my mum. "What on earth were you thinking, letting her go gallivanting around those camps? They're no place for a young girl! I've seen some of those young foreigners, hanging about the pubs, knocking back the alcohol."

As if I made a habit of it! My mum pulled a face at me behind Dad's back. She'd already met Madalina and liked the look of her, and approved of us helping with the uniform. She has a bit more faith in me than Dad has, apparently.

I wished I'd never brought up the subject. But Dad was well on his high horse now.

"You will *not* – repeat, *not* – go near that place again! You hear me, Amber?"

He thumped his fist on the table, hard enough to make the crockery rattle and cause my little sister Lucy to look up startled from watching Shaun the Sheep. Hamlet does not like raised voices and retreated behind the sofa. My dad repeated, "You hear me?" a little louder in case I'd missed it the first two times.

I got up. "Yes, Dad, perfectly," I said coldly, and restrained myself from adding that probably the whole street could hear him too. I'd never have said a word if I'd known he was going to kick off like that. I thought darkly that it's people like him who could be at the root of racial discrimination.

Normally I'd have picked up Hamlet and gone to my

room, "flouncing off" as my dad calls it. This time I tried clicking at him in imitation of Madalina's uncle, but he just sat there with his head on one side and looked puzzled. Evidently I didn't have the gift.

I left him there and stalked off on my own with as much dignity as I could muster.

two

Anyway, this episode was soon pushed into the background, because my elder sister Kim phoned and said she was coming home from uni for a week or so. This was unusual, and apparently all was not well. Not that I was told anything, as usual, but I caught snatches of conversation from behind my parents' closed bedroom door. They do an awful lot of talking behind that door, and mostly it's about one or other of us kids. Well, I suppose with five of us there's always something to discuss about somebody. I wish they'd be more *open* about it though, and not so secretive. If I want to know anything I have to dawdle on the landing and pretend I'm going to the bathroom if one of them opens the door. I have to pick up most of the family info that way. I'm sure other families sit around the table and talk about any problems in a civilised way.

I mentioned this to them once, and I got a typical

reply from my dad. He said "Well, I don't think this would work in our present family set-up. Lucy is only five, so she'd probably put her head on the table and fall asleep from sheer boredom. And you make such a drama out of everything that it would make things 10 times more complicated!"

Well! As if! So, as I said, I have to glean small snippets of info in passing, so to speak.

Anyway, what I heard about Kim was slightly alarming. I distinctly heard my dad say, "I think there's more to this than she's saying." My mum murmured something I couldn't catch, but I could tell she was using her worry-mode voice.

I've always been a little in awe of my sister Kim. She's seven years older than me, very clever and very beautiful. I used to look up to her a lot and think I'd be just like her when I grew up – long blonde hair, tall, athletic and full of energy. It hasn't quite worked out like that, with me being brown-haired, on the small side and pretty average in other ways. I remember her being nice to me when I was very little, and then a time when she wasn't so nice – it must have been when she was in her teens and I started playing around with her make-up and hanging about when her friends came round. Then she went away to uni to study sports science and we haven't seen all that much of each other since. I was really looking forward to her coming home.

It was a bit of a shock when she arrived though, Dad meeting her off the late train Friday evening. She came in out of the darkness wearing a red jacket and long scarf, flung her rucksack into a corner of the hall and smiled wanly at us all. She looked thinner, with dark smudges under her eyes as though she hadn't been sleeping properly.

"Are you OK, love?" asked Mum, worry-mode voice again, going to hug her. Kim hugged Lucy and me too. She's never been a skinny girl but not plump either; athletic would be the word, and very fit and toned from working out at the gym. Now she seemed frailer and thinner.

"I'm fine, Mum, just fine," she said, with the merest hint of impatience that sent out signals saying, "Don't fuss."

She didn't seem fine at all though. I'd remembered her as having a hearty interest in food, eating healthily and sensibly. Now she seemed uninterested in eating, picking at her supper and leaving some of it. Her face looked pale now that the summer tan had faded, and her hair was pulled back any old how. She seemed nervous and edgy and nearly jumped out of her skin when Hamlet suddenly had a nightmare and gave a loud yap in his sleep. Something was up, that was for sure.

After supper she pulled out a packet of cigarettes and a lighter. We were all a bit startled. "I didn't know you smoked," said Dad.

Kim lit up and inhaled deeply. "It's just occasional. I find it relaxes me. I'll go outside if you'd prefer."

"Well, if you don't mind, we would really," said

Mum, flapping away the smoke with the tea-towel as she got up to clear the table. I hate cigarette smoke and tried not to cough. When Kim came back, I noticed her hand tapped nervously on the table, and that her dark nail varnish had a few chips.

"Thing is, I'm thinking of chucking uni," she said at last, when we'd mentioned all the bits of local news we thought might interest her. A ripple of alarm went round the table. Mum said, "Oh dear!"

Dad said, "But you're just at the start of your final year. You've been doing so well. You can't let all that effort and work and money go to waste."

Typical Dad. Trust him to think mainly in terms of money when his daughter is obviously in some deep emotional need! I know he and Mum really sacrificed for Kim's and the boys' education, but this was surely not the time to point it out. He was looking rather worried though, and Mum said, "Has something gone wrong, love?"

Kim gave a shrug. She said, "Kind of."

"Is it to do with your studies?"

"Not exactly. Although I can't seem to concentrate properly any more."

"Then what? A relationship?"

"Kind of." They were really having to work hard to get anything out of her. Kim looked rather pointedly at me and then at Lucy. "Maybe I'll tell you more later. You know, when there aren't kids about."

I sat bolt upright at that. Who was she calling a kid? A sharp retort was on my tongue, but I bit it back when

I saw the utterly wretched look on her face. Whatever could the trouble be?

My mind was in overdrive but I'd have to wait. Kim sat moodily while Mum and I cleared up and Dad sat down with Lucy to watch the Simpsons. I was still smarting a little at being classed as a kid nearer Lucy's age than Kim's. I was quite surprised that she didn't object when Mum said we'd be sharing a room, as Lucy had moved into her old one.

After I'd done my homework I said I was getting an early night. They'll talk with me out of the way, I figured, and I might, I just might, be able to catch a little of the conversation if I happened to be loitering in the upstairs passageway.

Dad has me sussed out though. Ten minutes after I'd gone upstairs, leaving my bedroom door open a crack, he came to the foot of the stairs and called out pointedly, "Goodnight Amber! Sweet dreams!" And then went into the sitting room, closing the door very firmly behind him.

When Kim came to bed quite a while later I was still up, discussing things with a couple of the girls on Chatspace. We were planning to get together to make arrangements for our fashion show night. Kim threw her bag on the other bed, and then I saw her glance at the screen and frown a little.

"Is that a social networking site?"

I looked up, surprised. I'm not used to someone else coming into my room and I'd half-forgotten Kim was home.

"Yes, just chilling with the girls."

"I didn't know you were on Chatspace. You want to be careful."

I was even more surprised. "What do you mean?"

"Well, like I said, be careful. Don't ever link up with someone you don't know. And never give out where you live, or your address, or even what school you're at."

"Do you think I'm stupid?" I was indignant now. Did she think I was still some little kid, too ignorant to know my way round cyberspace? I shut down my laptop and got into bed. Kim didn't say any more but she seemed twitchy, unpacking and hanging up her stuff, making sure that the window was closed and the curtains drawn right across. I'd half-hoped she'd talk to me, in our room with the lights out, but I could see she wasn't going to. She got undressed, climbed into bed and switched off the light. I was still huffy and didn't try to make conversation. She obviously considered me far too young to confide in. Well, see if I cared!

I did care though, and wanted to connect in some way before going to sleep. After a bit, I whispered, "Kim, are you awake?"

No answer. She was either asleep, or wanted me to think she was. I sighed, turned over, and tried to sleep myself. I was just beginning to doze off when I heard a sound from the other bed. A kind of sniff, and then something that just might have been a smothered sob.

three

It must have been sometime in the small hours when I was woken suddenly by a strange sound. A kind of series of small strangled gasps, not loud but desperate-sounding, and some threshing about from the other bed. I recognised at once what was happening. I'd had the same kind of experience, screaming in my sleep during a bad dream and waking to find myself making those little strangled sounds. Kim was having a nightmare.

I switched on the bedside lamp and looked across. Her face was damp with sweat and she was breathing hard. I said, "Kim, Kim, wake up! You're dreaming. It's just a bad dream."

She opened her eyes with a dazed look, first puzzled, then relieved. "Oh! Sorry, did I wake you?"

"It's OK. What was it about?"

She sat up and pushed back her hair. I saw that her hands were trembling. Then she pulled her knees up under the duvet, dropped her head on them and began to sob quietly.

All of a sudden I couldn't bear it. I had a mental flashback, of me at about seven or eight, having a bad dream and climbing into Kim's bed for comfort. She'd always cuddled me and let me stay there. Now I climbed out of bed and went over to hers and got in beside her. She didn't push me away, but moved over a little to make room. Then she gave a kind of gulp, and said, "Oh, Ambie, I don't know what to do."

Ambie, that was what she used to call me when I was little. All of a sudden I wanted to cry too. I put my arms around her and said, "Kim, please, please tell me what's the matter."

She gulped and sniffed a couple more times, fumbled for a tissue to mop up, and said, "OK. But switch off the light and talk quietly. I don't want Mum and Dad hearing."

It was kind of cosy, lying there in the dark, cuddled up to my big sis and talking in whispers. She said, "I don't know where to start."

"Was it a boyfriend?" I prompted.

I felt her nod, and then shake her head. "Yes. No. Not really. It was this guy I met on the Internet, on Chatspace."

She sniffed another couple of times, blew her nose, and said, "It was so stupid. But he seemed so – normal. He asked for a link with me, said he was a student too and was looking for friends."

"And?"

"Well, we chatted for a few weeks, just ordinary stuff. Then he said he was coming to my town, might even take a look at the uni as he was thinking of changing courses and maybe I could show him around."

"Oh Kim, you didn't agree to meet him?"

"I did. Megan, my best mate, said I was stupid, so I told him I'd changed my mind."

I waited, holding my breath. She went on, "He seemed just ordinary, quite nice in fact. My age or a bit older. Not bad looking, in a geeky kind of way. Wore glasses. A bit intense maybe, from his messages. I didn't fancy him or anything."

"And then what?"

"Well, I thought that would be it, after I'd told him I'd changed my mind about meeting him. But he still kept on asking if I could show him round uni. I said he ought to make proper arrangements through the usual channels. He wanted to know where I lived but I didn't tell him. Didn't give him my phone number or anything."

"Oh Kim, no, of course you didn't!"

"But I did feel a bit sorry for him. Kept sending messages, seemed to be a bit lost, didn't know anybody. At first I replied, then I stopped replying and the messages got worse and worse, until he threatened he was going to try to find me! I started to feel a bit scared. I didn't want him to know where I was living. So I thought I'd ring Megan and ask her what to do. She suggested I come home for a bit."

"Oh, Kim!"

"I know. I've brought it all on myself. I wish I'd never started chatting to him."

I was trembling myself now. "Kim, he didn't ever find out where you lived, did he?"

"No, no. Yesterday I told him I didn't want him to send any more messages. I said, 'I'm sorry. I thought we might be friends but it hasn't worked out. So let's leave it at that.' And then he really freaked. Sent so many messages, I can't believe the whole Internet didn't crash!"

I felt my heart stop for a moment. "Kim, what . . . what did you do?"

She actually gave a little gaspy laugh. "I turned off the computer. And I came home."

She was quiet for a moment, so quiet that I could hear the ticking of the alarm clock by my bed.

"That's terrible!"

"Yep. And it's my own stupid fault. But it's messed up everything. I can't concentrate on work any more. I just want to leave uni and get away."

"Have you told the police?"

"Megan said I should, but I don't know – they'll say I asked for it, and after all, it's only messages, he doesn't have any way of getting my address. And Amber, I only told Mum and Dad half a story, if that. They just think I've had a bad break-up and I'm depressed. I couldn't say about the Internet. I feel I've let them down, let myself down."

"Oh, Kim!" I didn't know what to say, so I just hugged her tight. Suddenly it seemed that she was the child and I the older one. She must have had the same idea, because she said, "I must say you've grown up a lot, Ambie. You're not a kid any more." She sighed, and said, "I wish I knew where to go from here. I don't know what to do. I dread looking at my PC. D'you know, I'm almost afraid he saw me get on the train and followed me home. Stupid, isn't it?"

A shiver ran down my spine. But all of a sudden I knew what we must do. "Look, Kim, I think the police should be told. First thing tomorrow. But for now, we can pray. God knows all about the situation and he'll help."

She gave an incredulous little laugh. "God? My goodness, you really believe all that stuff, don't you? I thought all this church and club thing was just a phase you're going through."

"No," I said, "It's not. God is real, he helps me and he can help you."

I was quite surprised at myself, because I suddenly knew as I spoke out the words that I believed them, absolutely. "I'm going to pray," I said, and I did, there and then, in a whisper in the darkened bedroom, asking God to take charge of the whole scary situation and make things right for my sister again. She didn't say anything, but I could tell that tears were slipping down her cheeks once more. And a little later, I felt her relax beside me and could tell by her even breathing that she'd fallen asleep again.

four

It took me ages to go back to sleep. My mind was playing and re-playing the things Kim had told me. The whole thing seemed like scenes from some horror story.

And maybe it wasn't over yet. I held tight to the thought that God could sort it all out. And I even prayed for the saddo who'd been sending her messages.

In the morning, I overslept. Even so, Kim was still sound asleep, her cheek pillowed on her hand, looking beautiful and peaceful.

"Let her sleep," said Mum when I went downstairs. "Poor love, she's had an upsetting time of it."

And how, I thought, spreading strawberry jam on my toast.

All of us had planned to meet round at Willow's again. I took with me a few of my own clothes, a good denim miniskirt, a pair of jeans and a couple of tops. Of course Mum's eagle eye spotted the bag and asked questions, so I had to explain. Fortunately, she didn't disapprove.

"It's nice you're thinking of helping others," she said. "Just as long as you don't go expecting extra money from us to replace what you're donating."

As if! Honestly, parents don't give us much credit!

At Willow's, there were clothes everywhere, on hangers around the walls, draped over the furniture and piled on the bed. Everybody had their own opinions about what should be included in the sale and what should stay. My head was still full of Kim and her midnight confessions, and I longed to tell the girls the whole shocking story, scene by scene. But I'd promised not to say a word and I kept my promise.

After a while there was a knock on the front door.

Willow stuck her head out of the window and said, "Oh, it's Madalina. Ace! Come on up, Madalina," she called down.

The moment Madalina came in, we could see she'd been crying. Her eyelids looked swollen and her bottom lip was wobbling.

"Whatever's happened?" asked Chloe.

Madalina's lip wobbled some more, and then she covered her face with her hands and burst into tears. We cleared a small space among the chaos and sat her down. "Tell us," begged Annie.

"I have to leave!" sobbed Madalina, between gulps and sniffs.

"What, leave school?" said Willow, incredulously. "Why? What's happened? Has your uncle been making trouble?"

"No, no," said Madalina, mopping her eyes with the tissues Chloe handed her. "It's not that. We are all leaving. The work is finished for the season and we are going home. In one week's time. I have only one more week left in school."

The way she sobbed her heart out, you'd think the world had ended. We faffed about, saying stupid "there there" kinds of things that are no help at all really.

"But you'll be able to come back," said Willow, "when the next season's work starts. You'll be at school again then. And we'll stay in touch. We'll write to you all the time."

"Maybe you could take books back and learn at home," suggested Rachel.

"Maybe," said Madalina forlornly. "But it won't be the same. You are such good friends. Thank you."

We all trooped downstairs and made coffee to cheer ourselves up. Madalina did seem a bit brighter when we went back upstairs.

"Why are all your beautiful clothes pulled out like this?" she asked, waving her hand at the strewn and scattered garments.

Willow explained our plan, and added, "Oh yes, almost forgot. All of the others have chosen something for themselves, so you must do the same."

Madalina protested that she'd already been given so much, but Willow insisted and eventually she picked a long chunky cardi, perfect for cold winter weather. Then Willow had another thought. "We'd planned our fashion show for a couple of weeks' time, but if you're leaving in a week we ought to have it before you go. Maybe next Friday evening would be a good time."

"We could combine it with a leaving party for Madalina," said Rachel.

This idea bucked us all up and concentrated our minds. We'd have to get our skates on to get everything ready in less than a week.

"I will miss Beech Bank," said Madalina, on the verge of tears again.

"And Beech Bank will miss you," said Chloe. "You must come every single time next week. And bring your aunt to our epic fashion show!"

We had more or less sorted out what was to stay and what to go by the end of the morning. Madalina had left after an hour to meet her aunt at the Saturday market. We had a few more plans to mull over regarding a special send-off for her.

Back home for lunch, I found that Kim was up and about, chopping tomatoes at the kitchen table while Mum stirred chilli, by the smell of it. Kim looked well rested and cheerful, the big sister I knew and loved, with her hair freshly washed and shiny and the sparkle back in her eyes. A different girl to last night's nervous, brittle, edgy person.

"OK?" I said, and raised my eyebrows in a question.

She gave the merest jerk of her head towards Mum at the stove, and mouthed, "Later."

What on earth could have happened to create such a change? I couldn't wait to get her on her own. The chance came when the phone rang and Mum answered it. She stuck her head into the kitchen and said, "Stir the chilli, please, one of you. I'm taking this in the sitting room and might be a while. It's Grandma," she added with her hand over the phone. Kim and I both grinned. Grandma could never be called a woman of few words.

"What's happened?" I asked as soon as the sitting room door closed. "Something has, I can tell. You look totally different."

Kim finished chopping the tomatoes and slid them into the chilli mixture. "Yes, well, I'm beginning to think you might be on to something with this God stuff."

I stared at her. "What do you mean?"

"Well, you praying and all that. It seems to have worked."

"What's happened?"

"I've deleted my Chatspace account. I hope you don't mind, I borrowed your laptop. It was so simple, I don't know why I didn't do it before! Touch of a button and now Rodney can never bother me again!"

My head was trying to process this info and take in the surprising turn of events. It had certainly had an amazing effect on my sister, lifting the fear and stress that had been weighing her down. And she was giving the credit where it was due, to God!

"I'll just have to keep in touch with my friends in other ways. Mind you, I was stupid in the first place," she said, stirring the bubbling mixture in the pan. "And I hope you'll never, never do anything like that yourself, Amber."

"No Kim, I won't," I said meekly, and resisted the temptation to add, "As if!" She was back to regarding me as very much the little sister, it seemed. But it didn't matter.

She turned from the cooker and smiled at me. "I'm going for a run later. Want to come?"

"Yes, cool. But I think you should tell Mum and Dad. Everything. I think they should know, it's only fair. They do love us, really!"

Kim grinned at me and nodded. "You're right. I will."

I could hear Mum saying goodbye to Grandma, and Dad's car had just pulled up outside, delivering Lucy home from ballet class. They'd all be bursting in and private conversation would be out. I said quickly, "You'll be going back to uni then?"

"Yes. I'm not a bit scared any more."

I sent up a silent but heartfelt prayer.

five

We were all sad that Madalina would be leaving soon. We'd known she was only here for a while, of course, but she had become a real friend and part of our lives. That last week she worked as hard as ever at school, and came to Beech Bank with us every afternoon.

We were working hard at getting ready for the fashion show. We'd wanted to build a catwalk to run between rows of chairs in the big room, so that the models could twirl and the guests be able to see the clothes from every angle.

"Nothing worse than seeing something that looks good from the front but is fastened with safety pins at the back because it's too small, or folded over because it's too big," said Willow. But Rod and Sadie said they couldn't let us go parading about on some rickety construction that might be unsafe, and that if there was an accident, the Health and Safety people would be down on Beech Bank like a ton of bricks. So Annie's mum came up with a long red carpet runner and we settled for that. A dress shop in town had kindly loaned us a metal clothes rail, and someone had found a couple of dressmakers' dummies. Willow was in her element, arranging and draping things to their best advantage.

Madalina ran around fetching and carrying with the rest of us, a wistful look on her face. When Sadie decided it was time for a coffee break, I could see tears in Madalina's eyes again. Willow, her mouth full of pins, was arranging a velvet tunic on a dummy, and waved away the offer of coffee, but the rest of us sat down gratefully, clutching our mugs.

"We'll miss you, Madalina," said Sadie. "It's been so lovely getting to know you."

The tears were threatening to spill over, but Madalina gulped and said, "I will miss you too." She took a sip of coffee and I saw her eyes turn to the cross on the wall opposite the clock. "Will you . . . will you ask him to take care of me?"

Sadie followed her gaze. "You mean Jesus? Of course we will! But, Madalina, you can ask him yourself."

Madalina shook her head. "No, I don't know how. I know that he died, and that he came to life again, because you have told me. And I know it is true, because you speak to him and I can see that he is there with you. I can see he makes the big difference in your lives. But me, I am just a . . . a gypsy, and he may not have time for me. Not many do."

Several of us spoke at once, a chorus of voices assuring her that Jesus loved her every bit as much as any of us. Maybe more, because Sadie quickly grabbed her Bible and found a verse about God having a special regard for the outcast and the downtrodden. She leaned forward and took both of Madalina's hands.

"Madalina, Jesus loves you so very, very much. More than anyone else ever could. And he wants to be in your heart and life. He wants you to talk to him about everything that's on your mind. He wants you to let him love you."

"Truly?" Madalina's eyes were as big as saucers.

"Truly! Would you like us to pray with you, to ask him to come into your heart and your life?"

"Yes, I would! I would!"

And so we did, Sadie leading and all of us holding our mugs, and tears running down Madalina's cheeks as she realised that she now had her own place in God's kingdom for ever and ever.

She was truly a different girl, we could all see it for the rest of that week. The school uniform had made a big difference, but this was something that came from the inside, a knowing with certainty that God loved her and had accepted her into his family, and that she would grow into exactly the person God had planned for her to be.

The week went fast. Somehow, invitations went out, cakes were baked, decorations put up and everything prepared for the "Big Beech Bank showing of our Autumn/Winter Collection" as the posters grandly proclaimed. It turned out to be a cold, dark, damp, miserable kind of afternoon, but we were amazed and overwhelmed by the number of people who turned out. We'd agreed it would be a girls only affair; most

of us thought that if the boys came at all they'd come
with wrong motives, ogling and eyeing up the girls
rather than appreciating the fashion. So Rod and Hugh
had taken the BB boys off for an evening of go-karting,
and there was a granny on babysitting duty at the
Vicarage.

Annie's and Rachel's mums had both turned up, with
Rachel's sister Ruth. Chloe's Auntie Sue came along
too. Chloe said her aunt was really trying to understand
what was cool in teenage fashion, and she hoped she
would pick up a few more tips from the clothes she saw
here this evening. Madalina had got her aunt to come,
and there were a few other of the Eastern European
migrant women, standing shyly in a little bunch by the
door. Even Melanie Fisher had turned up, knowing full
well that it was a girls only event. Lots of the other BB
mums and sisters had come, too, including my own
mum and Kim.

Willow had seen me and Kim out together during
the week and had a brainwave. "Your sister's real model
material, tall and well fit. How about her modelling
some of the sporty stuff?"

So that's how we did it. There were three top models
– Sadie, thin as a rail, waif-like, for the floaty ethereal
stuff, Kim, in casual sporty gear, Willow, just drop-
dead elegant, with a kind of extra glow about her that
just *might* be something to do with the email she'd had
from Jay that morning. All three of them were brilliant,
strutting the red carpet, striking a pose with hand on hip,
giving a twirl, as to the manner born. Applause followed

their every appearance. The rest of us, as supporting cast, did the best we could, which was pretty average at best and near disastrous at worst. Chloe and Annie did pretty well, I managed to put my heel through the hem of a long skirt, which spoiled the effect somewhat, not helped by my red face. Rachel insisted on wearing three inch platforms to make her legs look longer, tripped on the edge of the carpet, tottered, and landed almost in the lap of someone's grandma. But it all rather added to the atmosphere rather than spoilt it, and everyone appeared to enjoy the show. The auction afterwards went at a cracking pace, almost every garment sold (I bought one or two things myself) and we couldn't wait to add up the money later.

At refreshment time, we did our best to see that everyone felt welcome, especially the migrant women. Madalina's aunt, Isabel, smiled shyly at me and said "Thank you" in English. Madalina herself seemed bursting with some excitement. "I have something to tell you," she said. "I want to tell all of you, all five together."

Getting all five of us in one place was something of a tall order, but we managed it later, when people were beginning to leave, clutching their purchases and thanking us for a lovely evening. We wondered what on earth could be up, looking at Madalina's pink cheeks and shining eyes.

"It is wonderful!" she burst out. "Today, at school, I was called to see the Head. He tells me that there is something – a bursary – that provides for pupils of exceptional promise." She paused and we held our breaths.

"And . . .?" prompted Rachel.

"And – it has been awarded to me! And to Bogdan. Because I have high IQ, and he is extraordinarily promising in the area of physics and science." She pronounced the long words carefully, a syllable at a time, evidently having memorised what was said word for word. "They pay for everything – lodgings, food – everything. I can stay at school!"

We all hooted and shrieked. What an amazing turn-up!

"And so you're staying?" asked Willow.

Madalina shook her head. "I go home now, to see my family and to talk to them about everything. But I will come back!" She repeated it, as though she could hardly believe it herself. "I will come back! And go to school!"

Well, we could hardly have asked for a better end to the evening. Madalina suddenly remembered something and produced a little basket. "I have gifts!"

We'd bought farewell presents for Madalina, books and girly things. We hadn't expected anything from her, and were touched when she handed out beautifully carved and painted small wooden objects – a tiny cup and saucer, intricately patterned plate, a doll-sized teapot, a little box.

"Did your family make these, Madalina?" asked Annie, turning the lovely little teapot over in her hands.

"Yes, my uncle did them all," said Madalina. "He is grateful for your kindness to me." She fished about in the basket and handed me my gift. It was a whistle, beautifully carved in a pale wood and painted in red with beautiful patterns of flowers and leaves. "This is for you, Amber. My uncle said it was for the girl with the dog. A dog will listen to the note of this whistle and come. Even with *gadja*."

I took the whistle and looked at it, a lump in my throat. It must have taken hours to decorate like that. And I'd suspected Madalina's uncle of all kinds of terrible things. I vowed I would never judge others hastily again.

"It's beautiful, Madalina," I said. "Tell your uncle thank you so much."

Not many people were left now, and the Beech Bank folk were beginning to clear up. I stood for a while after Madalina and Isabel had left, holding the Romany whistle and feeling kind of humble and blessed. I might never be able to talk to dogs in the way the Roma did, but I was sure that Hamlet would always come to me when I blew this whistle. I couldn't wait to try it out.

In the meantime, there were bits of tinsel and paper to clear up, odd garments to sort, the red carpet to roll up, tables to clear, mugs to wash. Everything had to be spick-and-span for another week at the Beech Bank Club. You never knew what might be just around the corner!

Beech Bank Girls – Every Girl Has A Story
by Eleanor Watkins

Christian chick lit for ages 10–14. Six teenage friends draw nearer to God and to each other in these fun, moving and honest accounts. Annie, Willow, Rachel, Holly, Amber and Chloe share their laughter, their tears, their hopes, their fears and their secrets with each other and with us. Miracle and party included!

> "*Beech Bank Girls* is a very interesting book, dealing with a whole number of situations encountered by teenage girls. It portrays well the struggles the girls have and at the same time helps to show what to do in each situation. I would recommend this book as I really enjoyed it and found it helpful at the same time." – Claire

> "I loved reading about the different girls' lives and how they struggled with different problems at school, at home and with their Christian lives. It also teaches more about God, like how he knows each and every one of us, he loves us all, listens to us and will help us with everything." – Emma

ISBN 978 0 9536963 4 5

Deepest Darkness
by Denise Hayward

Ten-year-old Abi suffers from terrible nightmares and her life is ruled by fear. On holiday in Canada, she makes a new friend who shows her that true light shines, even in the deepest darkness. Facing her fears one by one, Abi opens up her life to the True Light and finds a freedom that she never thought possible. A gentle, moving story for 8–11s.

"This is a brilliant story all about a girl called Abi . . . this is one of the best books I have read – EVER!" – Maddie

"It is a fantastic adventure and God is really real." – Natalie

"I enjoyed the story very much. I felt for Abi and all the characters and was really excited while reading the book." – Polina

ISBN 978 0 9536963 6 9

Available from your local book shop, on-line book store or directly from www.dernierpublishing.com

I Want To Be An Airline Pilot
by Mary Weeks Millard

Shema, an eight-year-old Rwandan goatherd from a child-led family, has many adventures, including a goat eating his only T-shirt, a frightening visit to a medicine man and a dangerously close brush with a spitting black cobra! Through them all, little by little, Shema learns about "Mister God" and discovers that although he is an orphan, he has a Father in heaven who cares for him. A victorious, heart-warming story for 8–11s, with lovely background to life in rural Rwanda.

"I give this book 10/10." – Ellen

"A thrilling adventure story about three orphans' dreams coming true when their prayers were answered." – Jonathan

"I think this book is very good, it made me feel happy, sad and really excited. I think the most interesting part was when Shema faced the black cobra. It was also very moving when in the book Ishimwe starts to cry because her parents died. I really enjoyed this book, it is one of my favourites." – Kemi

ISBN 978 0 9536963 5 2

Available from your local book shop, on-line book store or directly from www.dernierpublishing.com

London's Gone
by J. M. Evans

London has been bombed by terrorists. Maria watched in horror as the smoke rose from the direction of London. Now she must make a hazardous journey to safety with her sister and a Christian friend, but is anywhere safe now? For Maria, the journey is also inside herself as she begins to discover a side to life that she did not know existed. A thrilling drama full of suspense. For ages 12+

"I just couldn't put this book down!" – Jilly

"I found the story very tense and compelling." – Sandy

"A roller coaster ride of adventure that I found difficult to put down. The characters were well developed and it was great to see how their relationships with each other changed and grew as the story went on. A great read and a book I would thoroughly recommend." – Jo

"Scary, because it could actually happen." – Laura

ISBN 978 0 9536963 2 1

Available from your local book shop, on-line book store or directly from www.dernierpublishing.com

The Treasure Hunt
by J. M. Evans

Ravi, Debbie, Joel and Lance's first exciting mystery adventure. Who is in the back of the white lorry and why are they there? Prayer, faith and their Bible knowledge all help, but when the case takes an unexpected turn, the friends also need to be courageous and obedient. Will they find out what is going on and find the real treasure? For ages 8–11.

"The best book I've ever read!" – Emily

"Brilliant!" – Ben

"This is a really good story. I couldn't stop reading it. I liked the mystery and it was full of suspense." – Lydia

"I couldn't wait for the next chapter. The people seemed real. I hope there will be more." – Matt

ISBN 978 0 9536963 1 4

Available from your local book shop, on-line book store or directly from www.dernierpublishing.com

Mystery in the Snow
by J. M. Evans

Not long after solving their first mystery (*The Treasure Hunt*), Ravi, Debbie, Lance and Joel find themselves with another problem: Ravi's shed has been burgled. Can they find out who did it? The plot thickens as an old lady's handbag goes missing, then a cat disappears. Can all these things be connected? Join the Christian friends as they find answers in unexpected places. For ages 8–11.

"So exciting that I couldn't put it down!" – Lydia

"There are some books that can be boring, but this book made me definitely want to carry on reading. I would definitely recommend it." – Joshua

"I really enjoyed reading *Mystery in the Snow* because I like mystery and Christian books and found this one very exciting, adventurous and mysterious. I like how it teaches that when people pray and obey God they can make a difference in people's lives. This story would appeal to people who like adventure and mystery books." – Emma

ISBN 978 0 9536963 3 8

Available from your local book shop, on-line book store or directly from www.dernierpublishing.com